ARF AND the GREEDY GRABBER

by Philip Wooderson

ILLUSTRATED BY BRIDGET MACKEITH
COLORS BY JESSICA FUCHS

Librarian Reviewer
Laurie K. Holland
Media Specialist (National Board Certified), Edina, MN
MA in Elementary Education, Minnesota State University, Mankato, MN

Reading Consultant
Sherry Klehr
Elementary/Middle School Educator, Edina Public Schools, MN
MA in Education, University of Minnesota, MN

STONE ARCH BOOKS
Minneapolis   San Diego

First published in the United States in 2006
by Stone Arch Books,
151 Good Counsel Drive, P.O. Box 669,
Mankato, Minnesota 56002.
www.stonearchbooks.com

Originally published in Great Britain in 2000
by A & C Black Publishers Ltd.

Text copyright © 2000 Philip Wooderson
Illustrations copyright © 2000 Bridget MacKeith

Library of Congress Cataloging-in-Publication Data
Wooderson, Philip.
    Arf and the Greedy Grabber / by Philip Wooderson; illustrated by Bridget
MacKeith.
      p. cm. — (Graphic Trax)
      ISBN-13: 978-1-59889-022-8
      ISBN-10: 1-59889-022-0
      1. Graphic novels. I. MacKeith, Bridget. II. Title. III. Series.
PN6727.W66A74 2006
741.5—dc22   2005026688

Summary: Arf loves to play practical jokes. His tricks give him and his sister a laugh
until one joke backfires, and he and his sister end up in trouble with the police.

1 2 3 4 5 6 11 10 09 08 07 06

Printed in the United States of America.

TABLE OF CONTENTS

THE GREEDY GRABBER

MRS. DUDLEY

ARF

MOM

GLORIA
(ARF'S OLDER SISTER)

BEE
(ARF'S LITTLE SISTER)

CHAPTER ONE

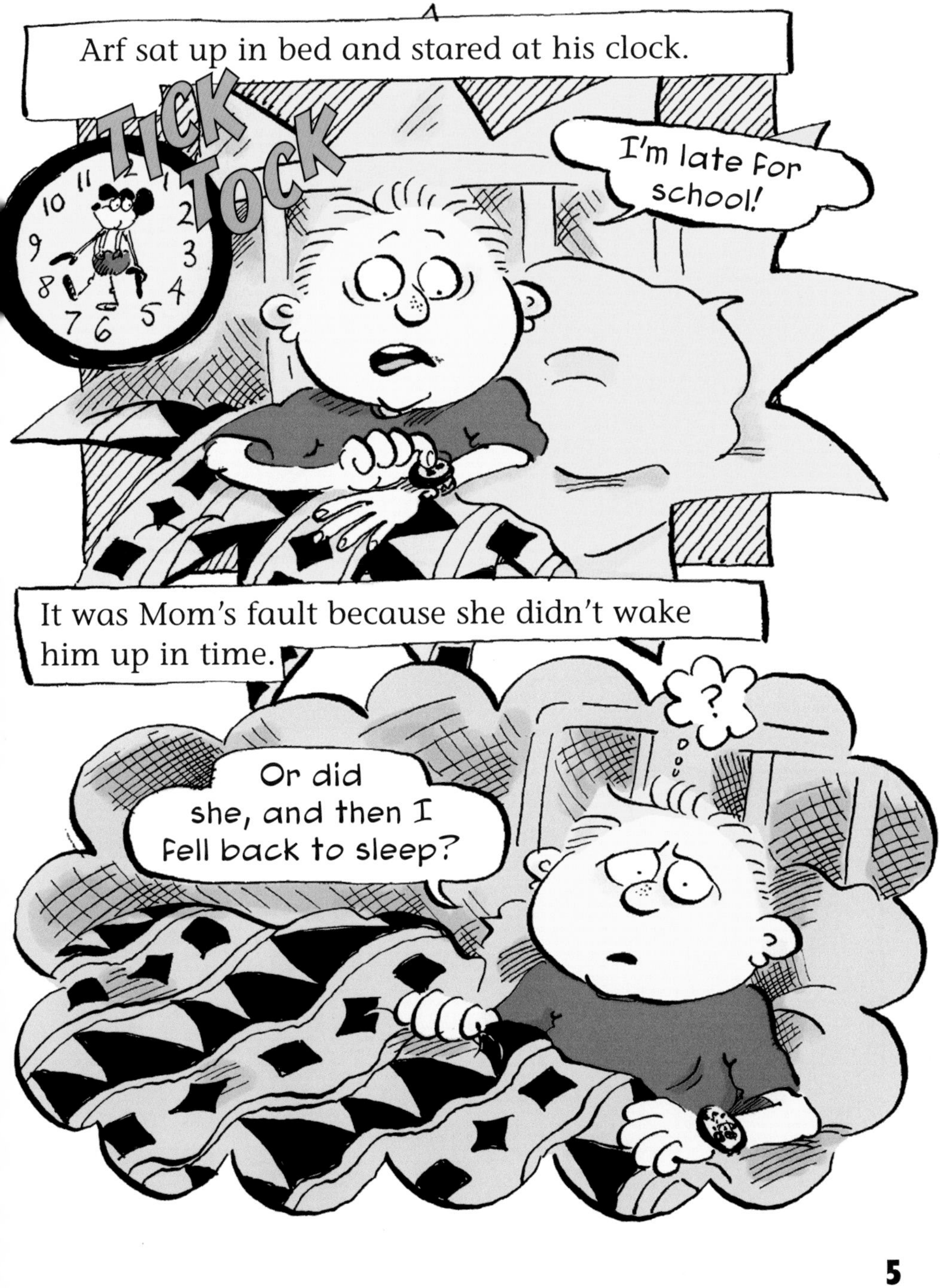
Arf sat up in bed and stared at his clock.
TICK TOCK
I'm late for school!
It was Mom's fault because she didn't wake him up in time.
?
Or did she, and then I fell back to sleep?

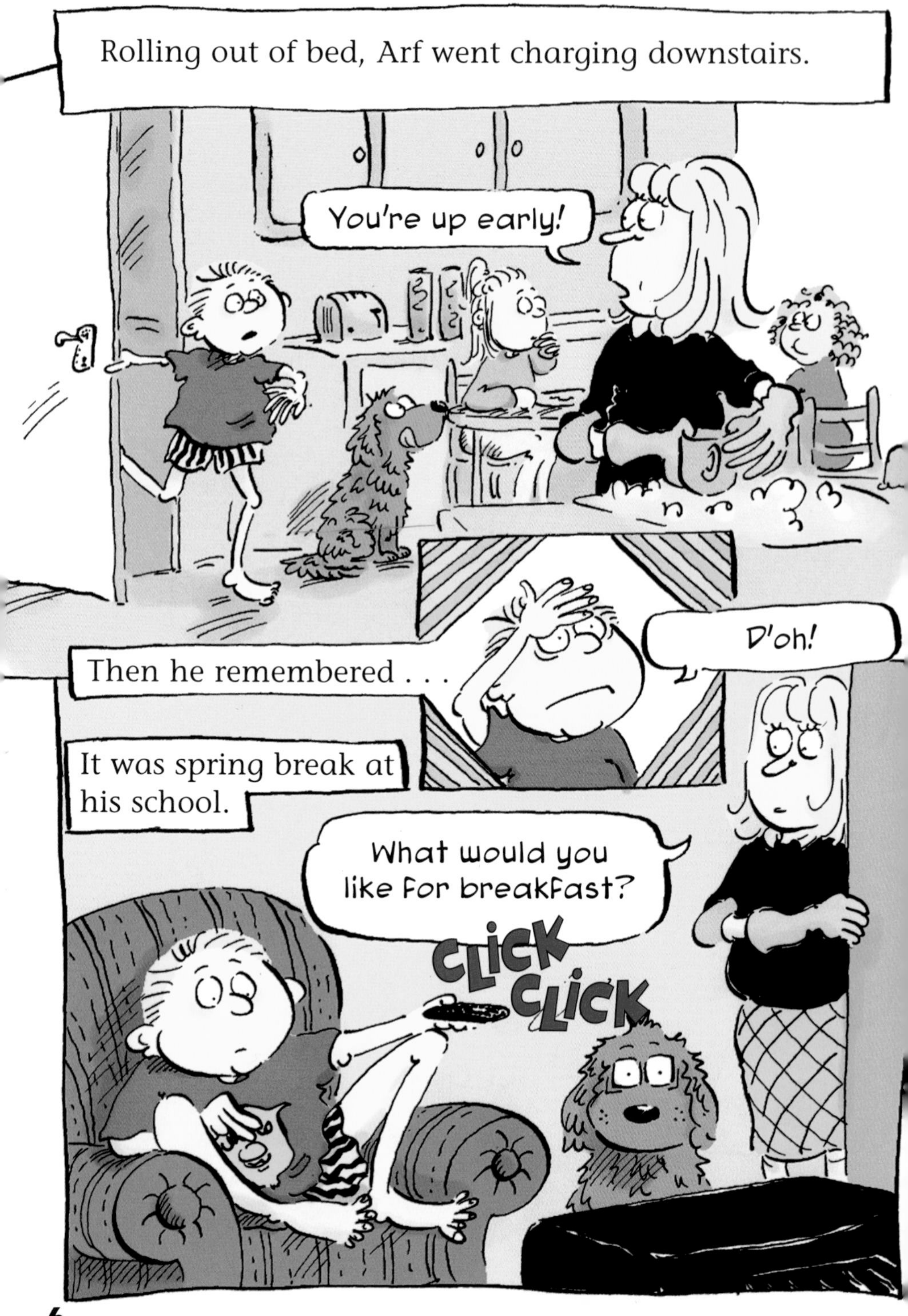
Rolling out of bed, Arf went charging downstairs.
You're up early!
Then he remembered . . .
D'oh!
It was spring break at his school.
What would you like for breakfast?
CLICK
CLICK

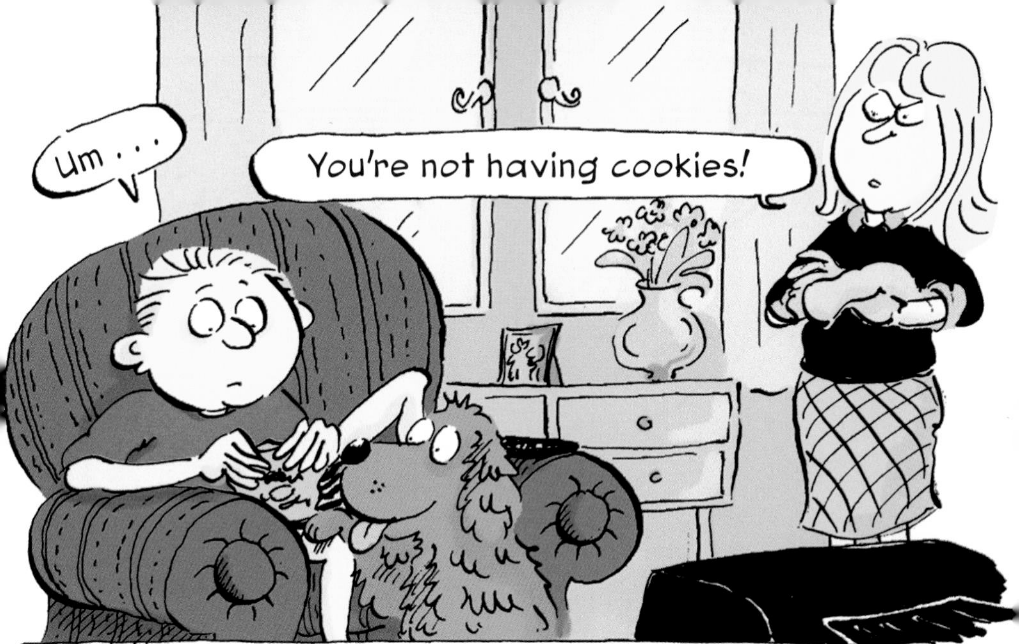
Um . . .
You're not having cookies!

Arf ended up gluing three slices of toast into a sticky sandwich with peanut butter and jelly.

“Oh yuck!” said Gloria. She was Arf’s older sister.

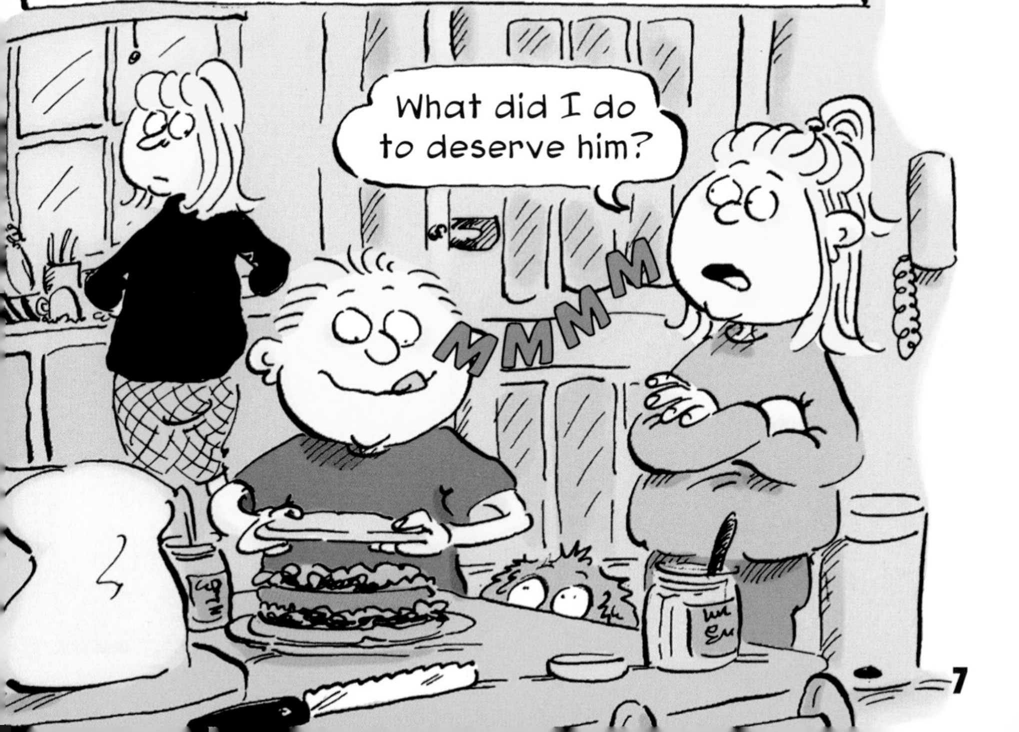
What did I do to deserve him?
MMMMM

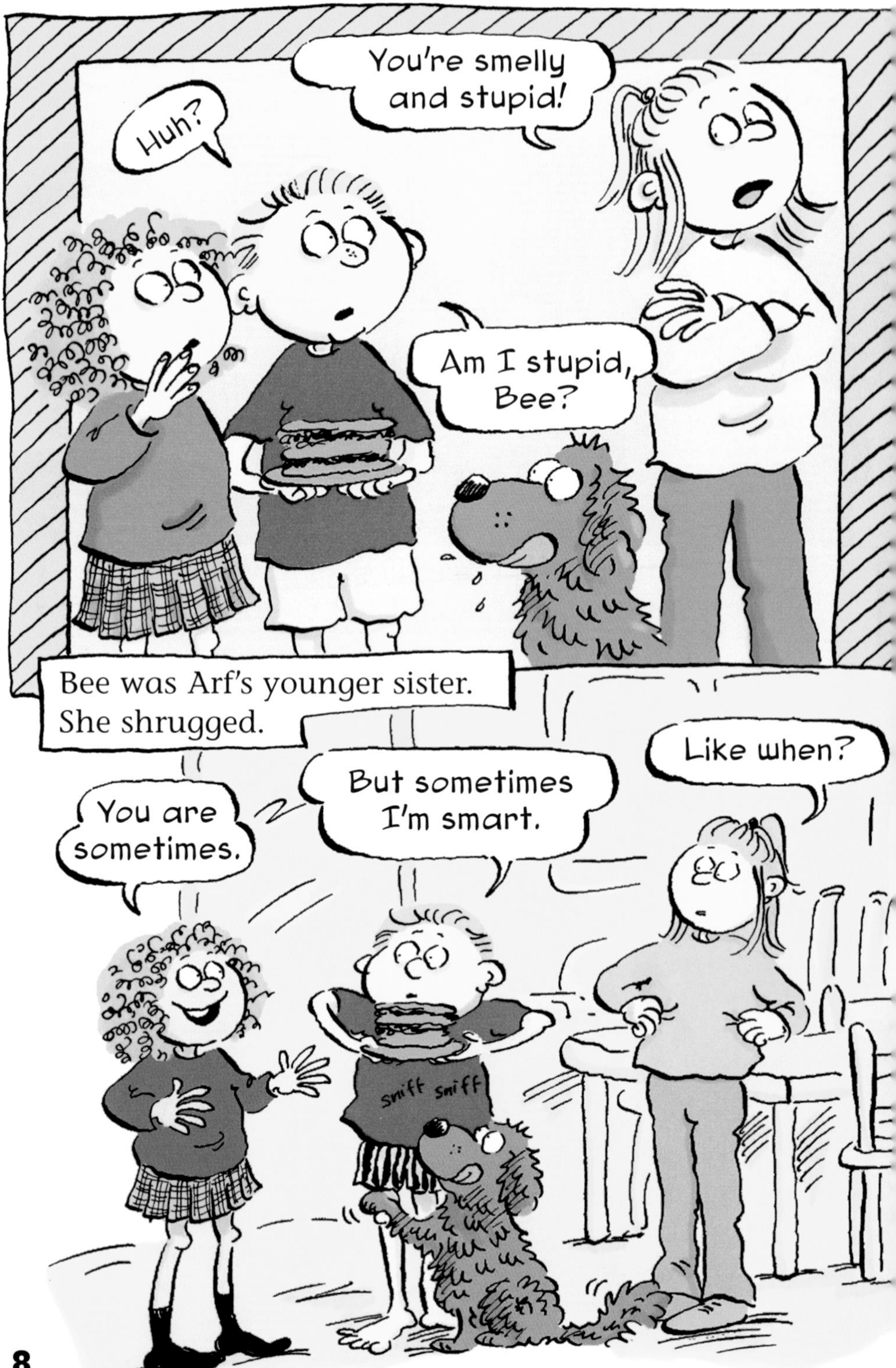
You're smelly and stupid!
Huh?
Am I stupid, Bee?
Bee was Arf's younger sister. She shrugged.
You are sometimes.
But sometimes I'm smart.
Like when?
sniff sniff

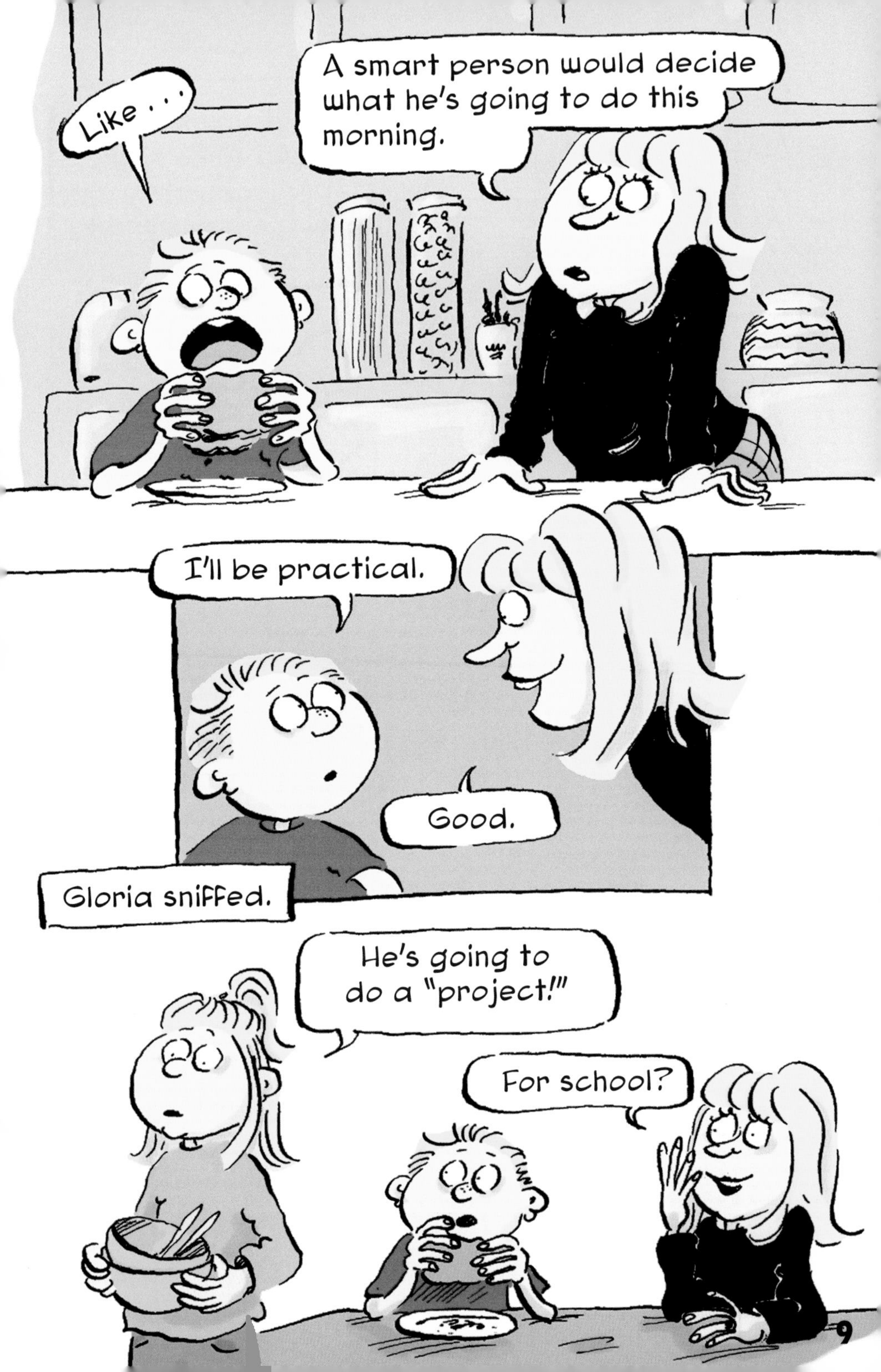
Like . . .
A smart person would decide what he's going to do this morning.
I'll be practical.
Good.
Gloria sniffed.
He's going to do a "project!"
For school?

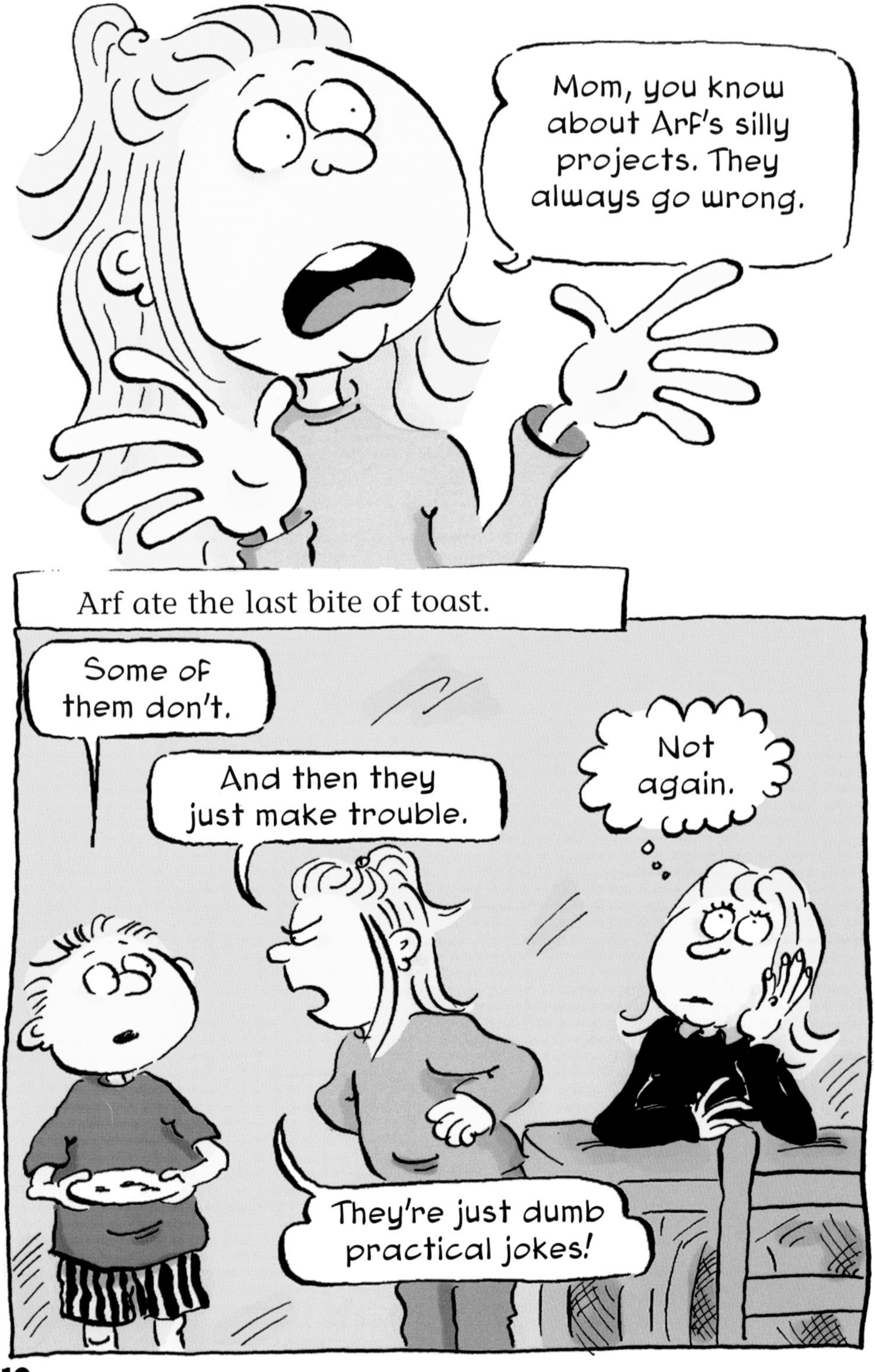
Mom, you know about Arf's silly projects. They always go wrong.
Arf ate the last bite of toast.
Some of them don't.
And then they just make trouble.
Not again.
They're just dumb practical jokes!

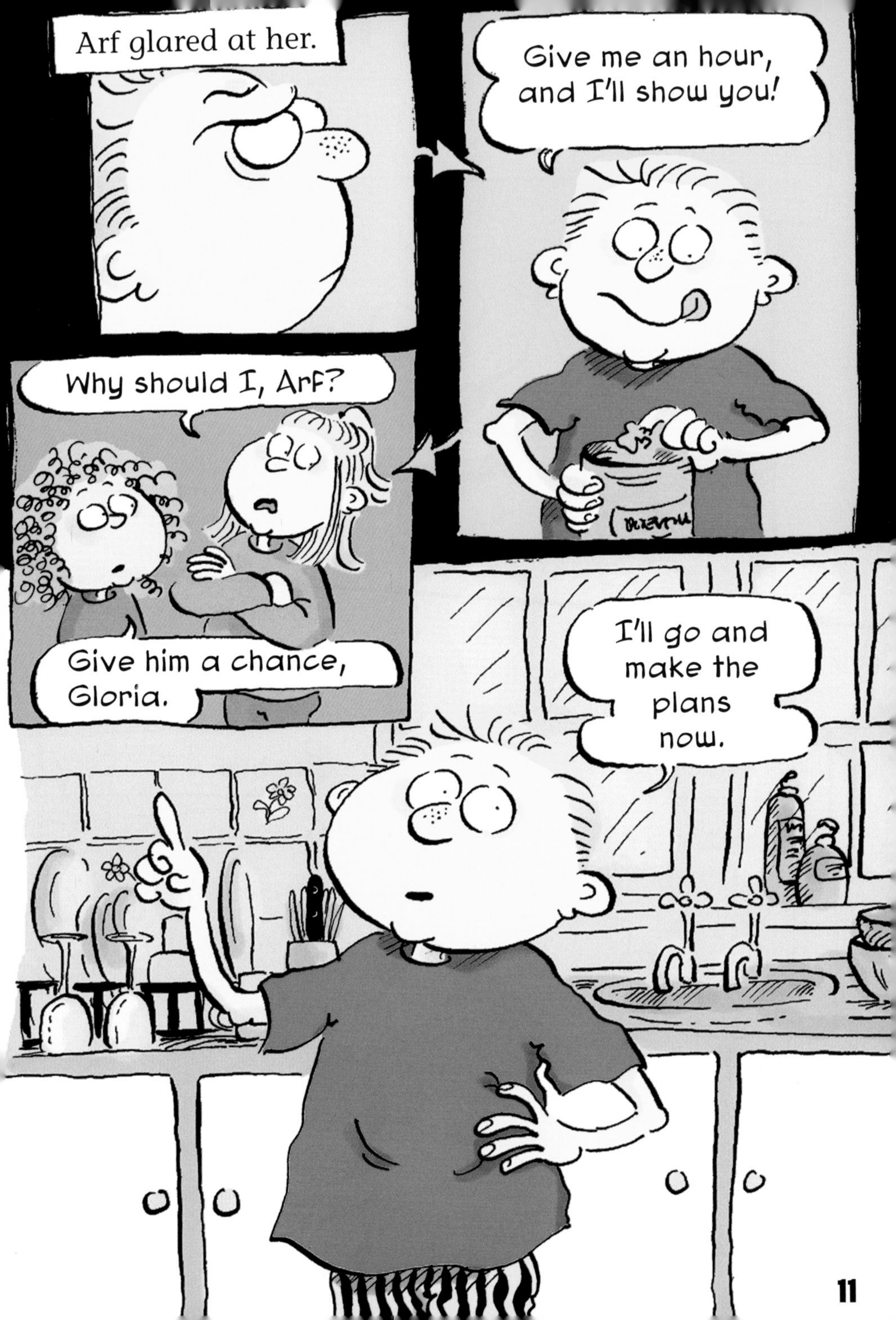

Arf glared at her.
Give me an hour, and I'll show you!
Why should I, Arf?
Give him a chance, Gloria.
I'll go and make the plans now.

CHAPTER TWO

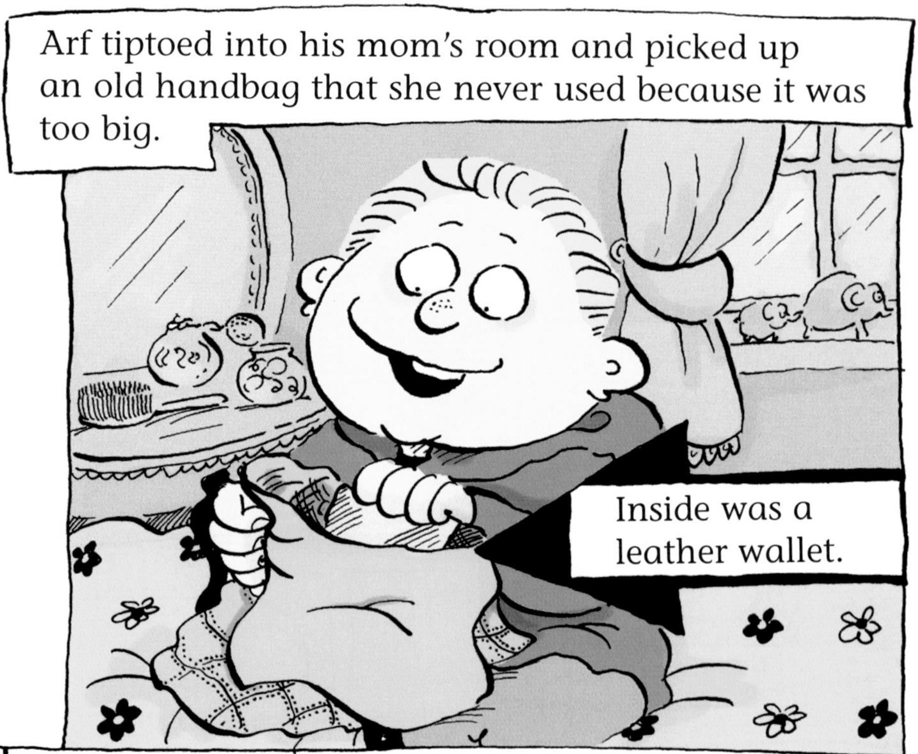
Arf tiptoed into his mom's room and picked up an old handbag that she never used because it was too big.
Inside was a leather wallet.

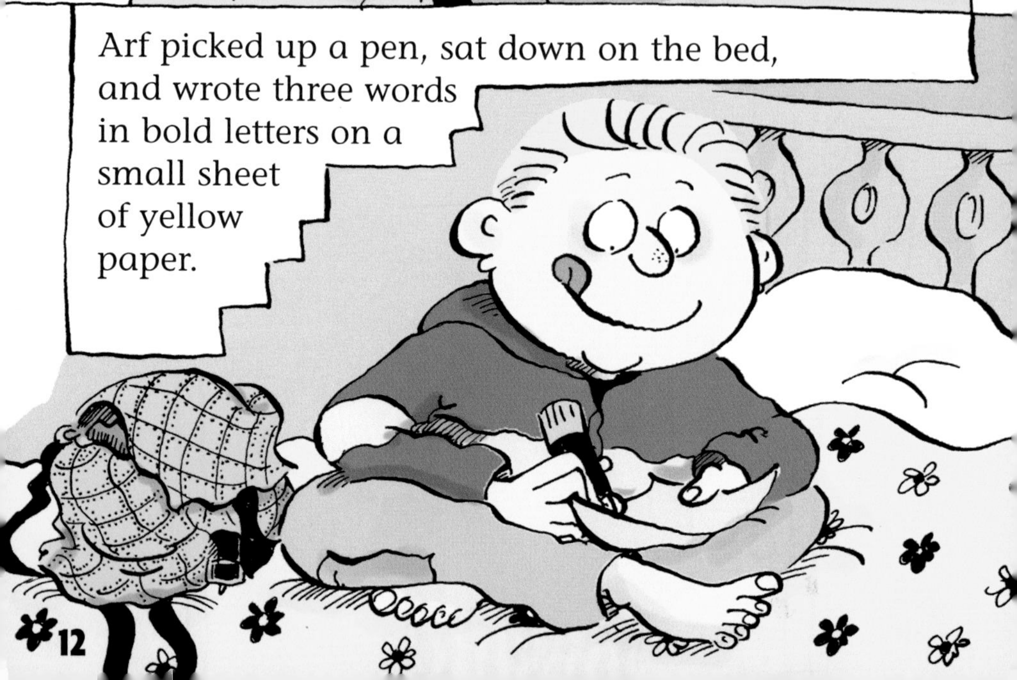
Arf picked up a pen, sat down on the bed, and wrote three words in bold letters on a small sheet of yellow paper.

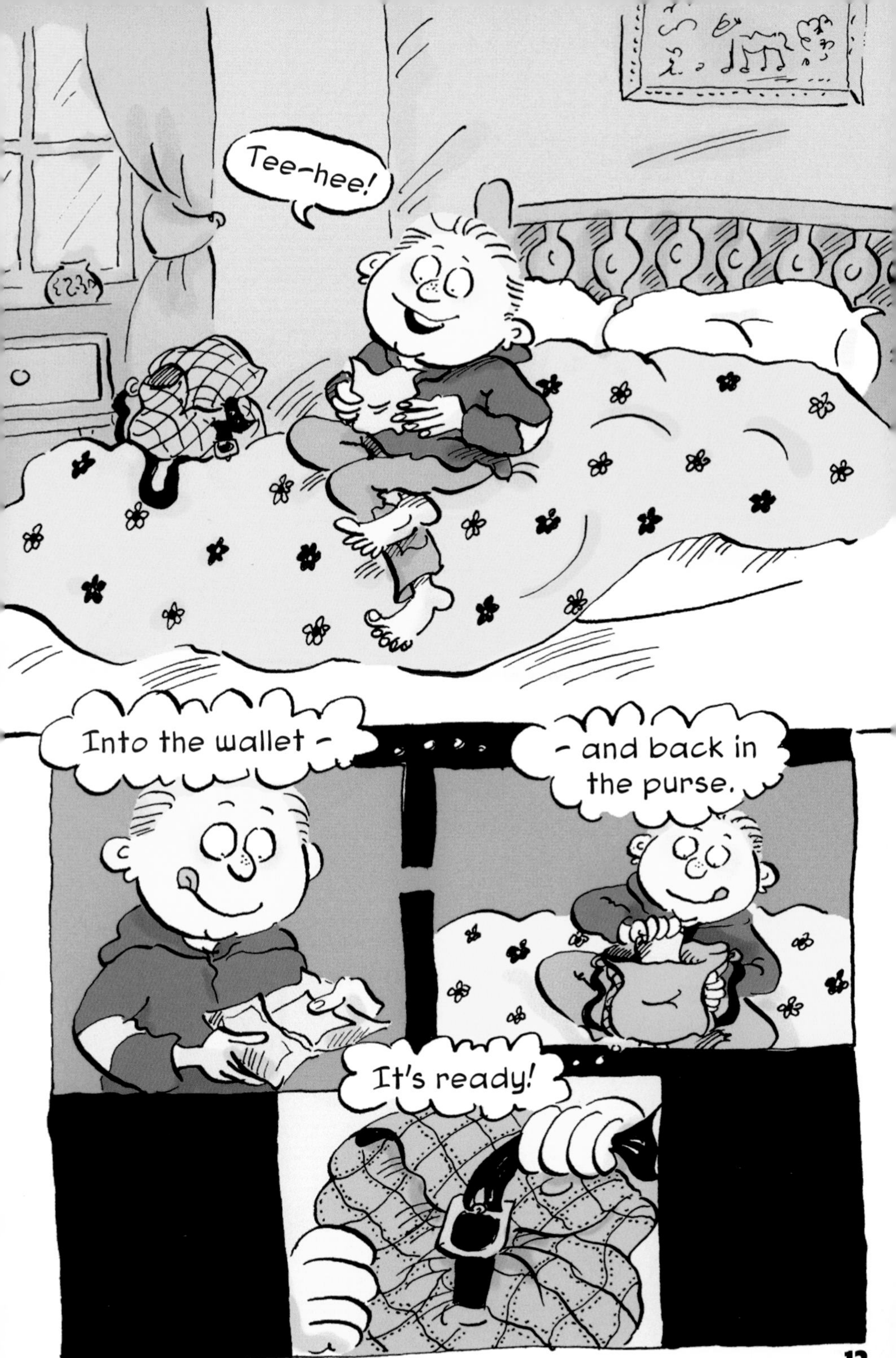
Tee-hee!
Into the wallet -
- and back in the purse.
It's ready!

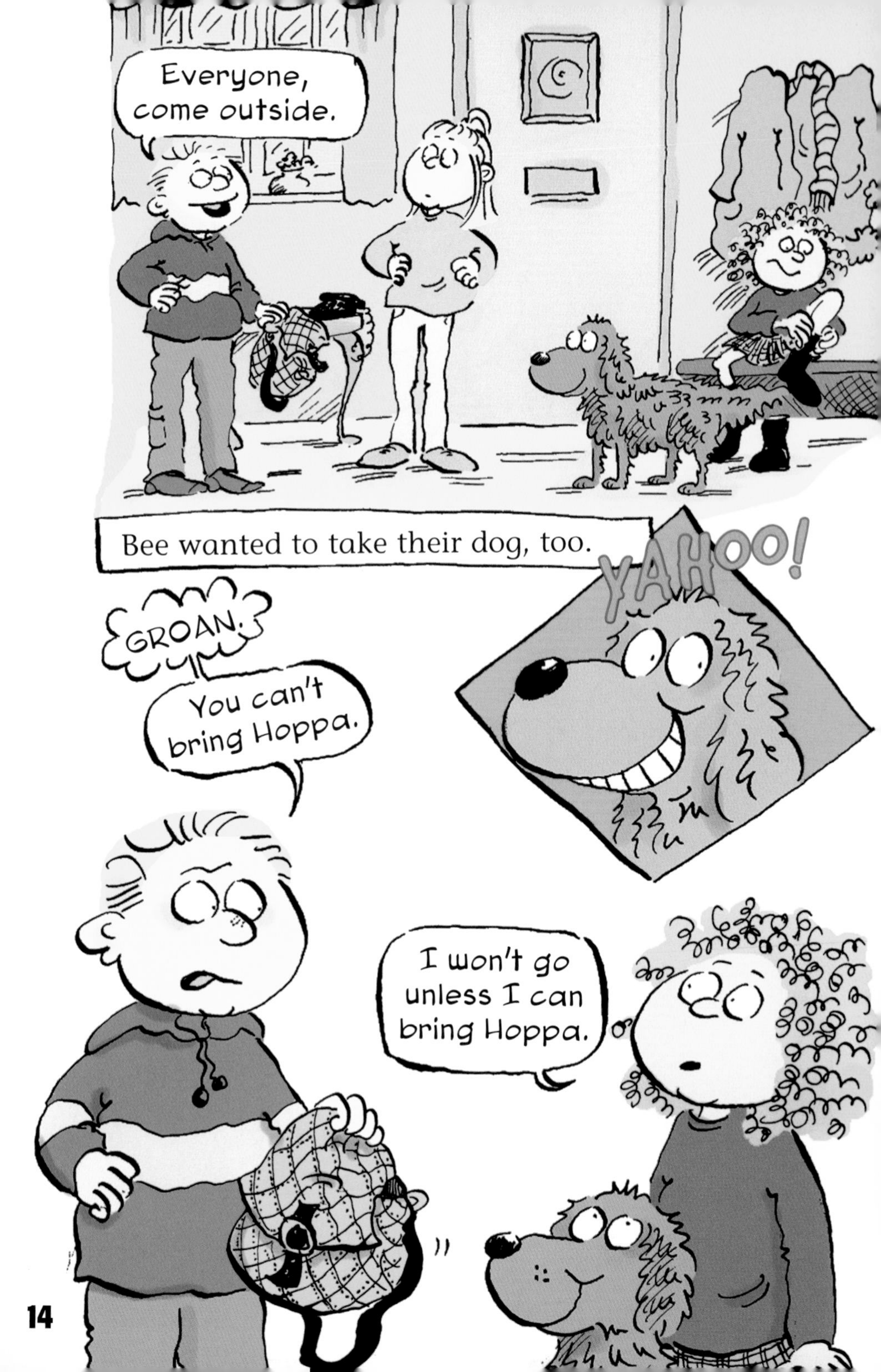
Everyone, come outside.
Bee wanted to take their dog, too.
YAHOO!
GROAN.
You can't bring Hoppa.
I won't go unless I can bring Hoppa.

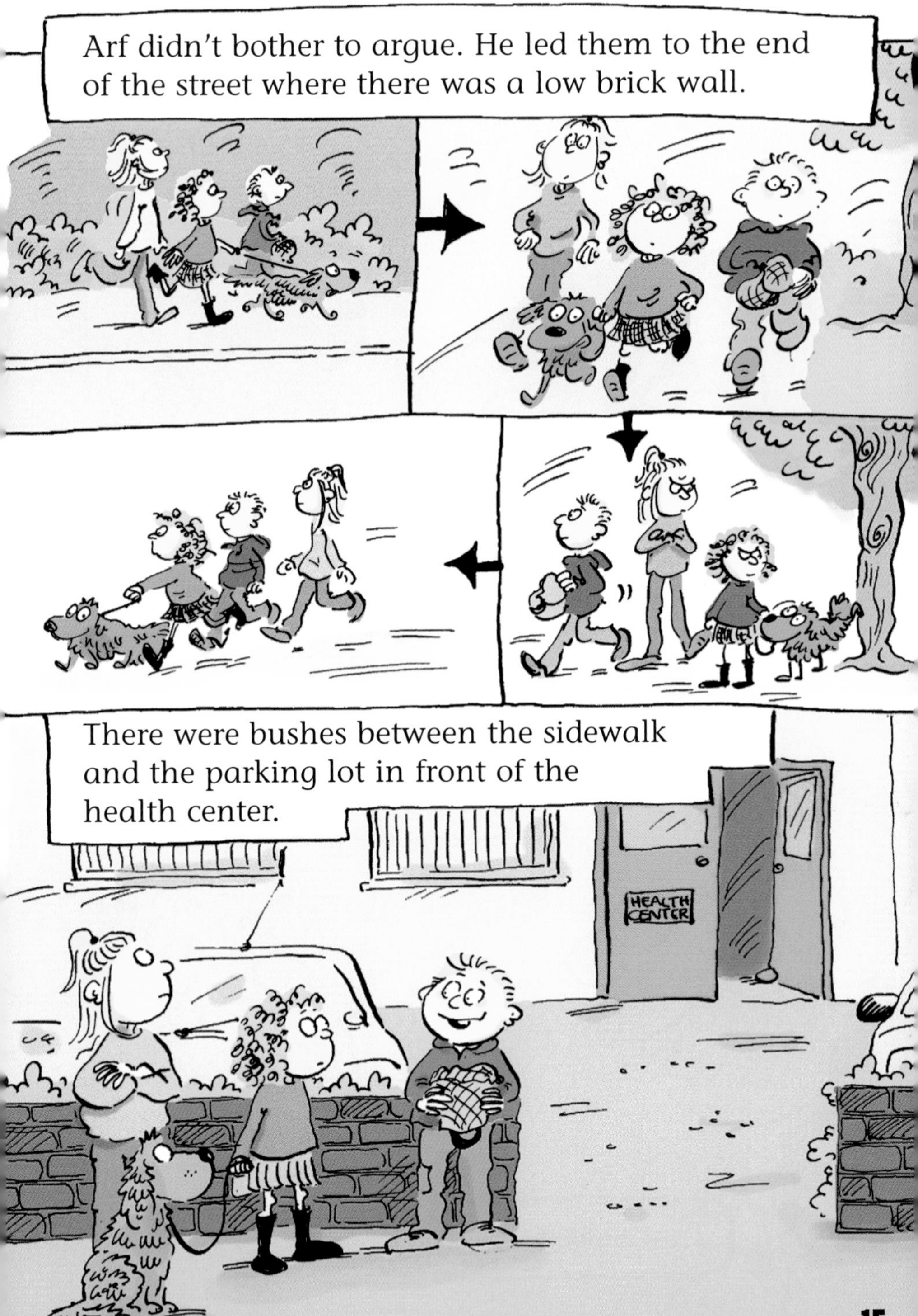
Arf didn't bother to argue. He led them to the end of the street where there was a low brick wall.
There were bushes between the sidewalk and the parking lot in front of the health center.
HEALTH CENTER

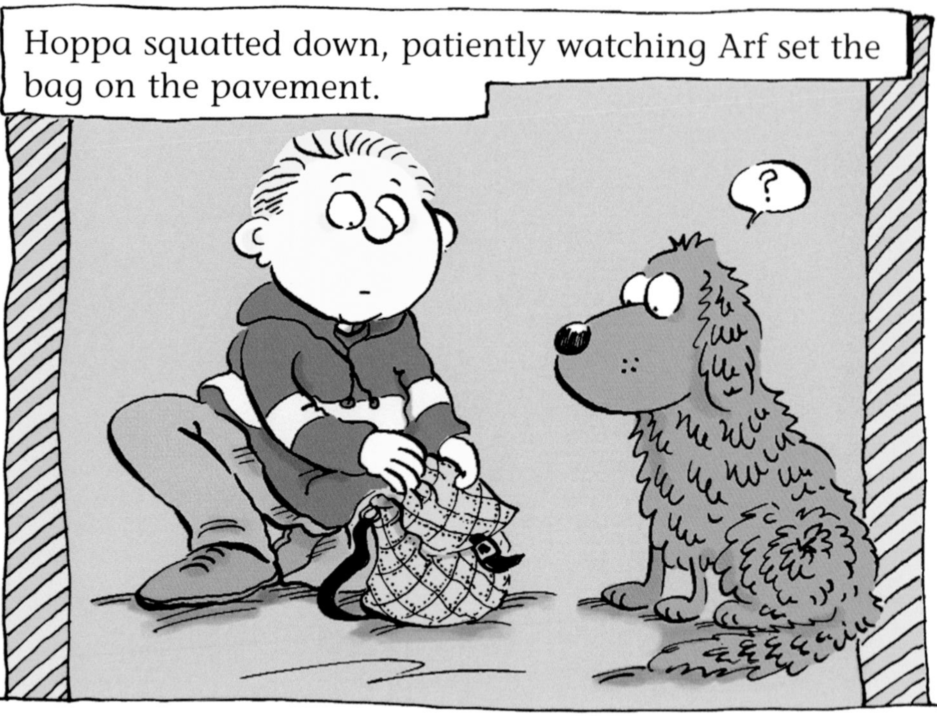
Hoppa squatted down, patiently watching Arf set the bag on the pavement.
?

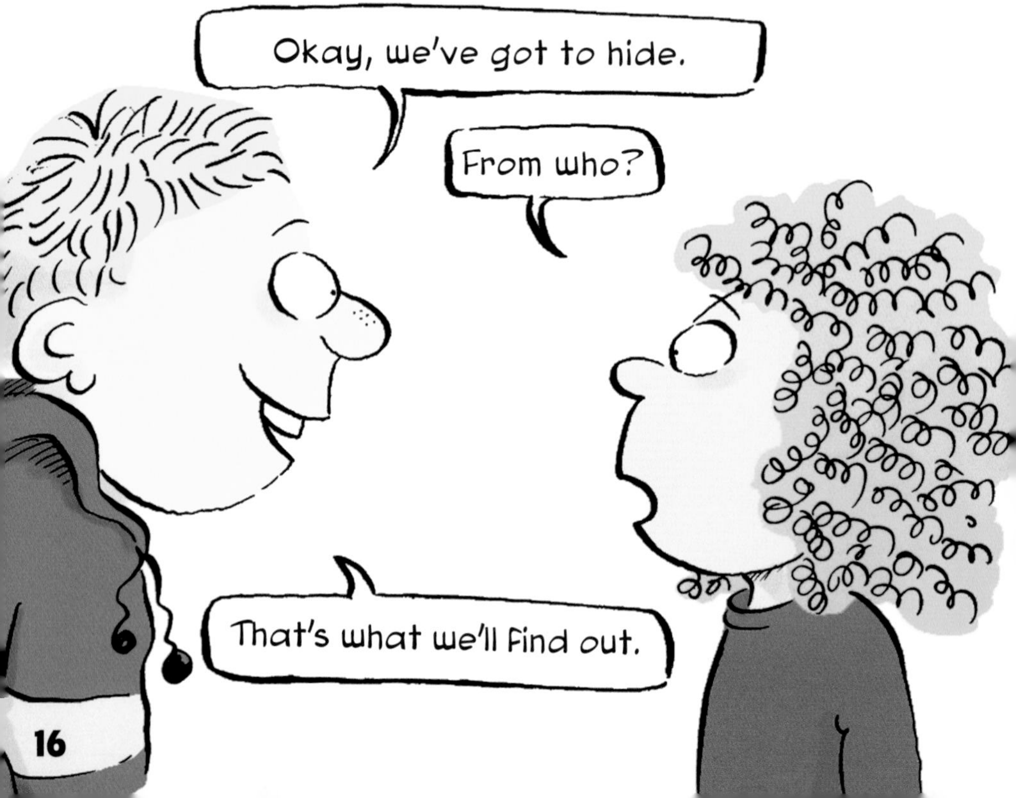
Okay, we've got to hide.
From who?
That's what we'll find out.

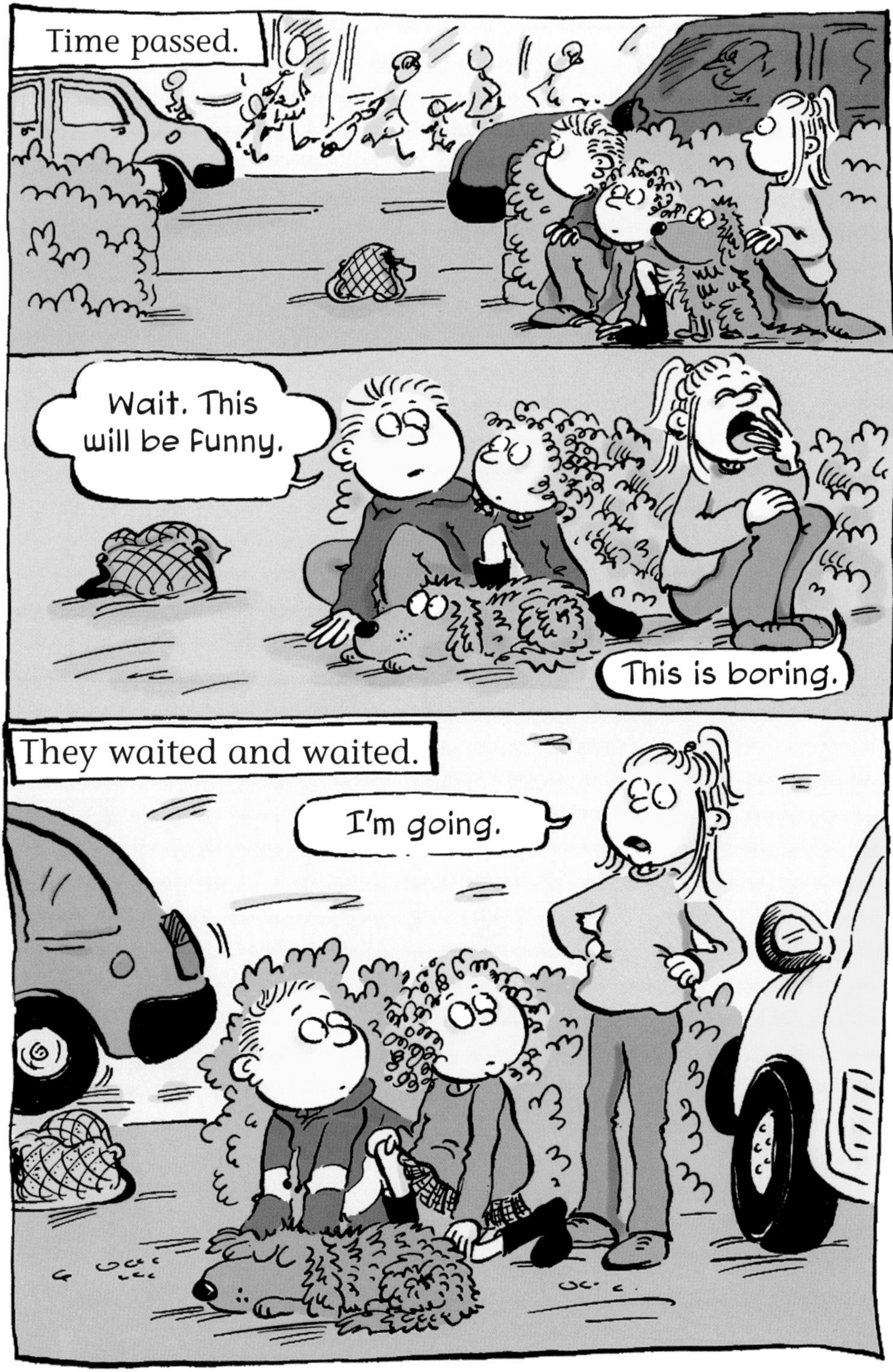
Time passed.
Wait. This will be funny.
This is boring.
They waited and waited.
I'm going.

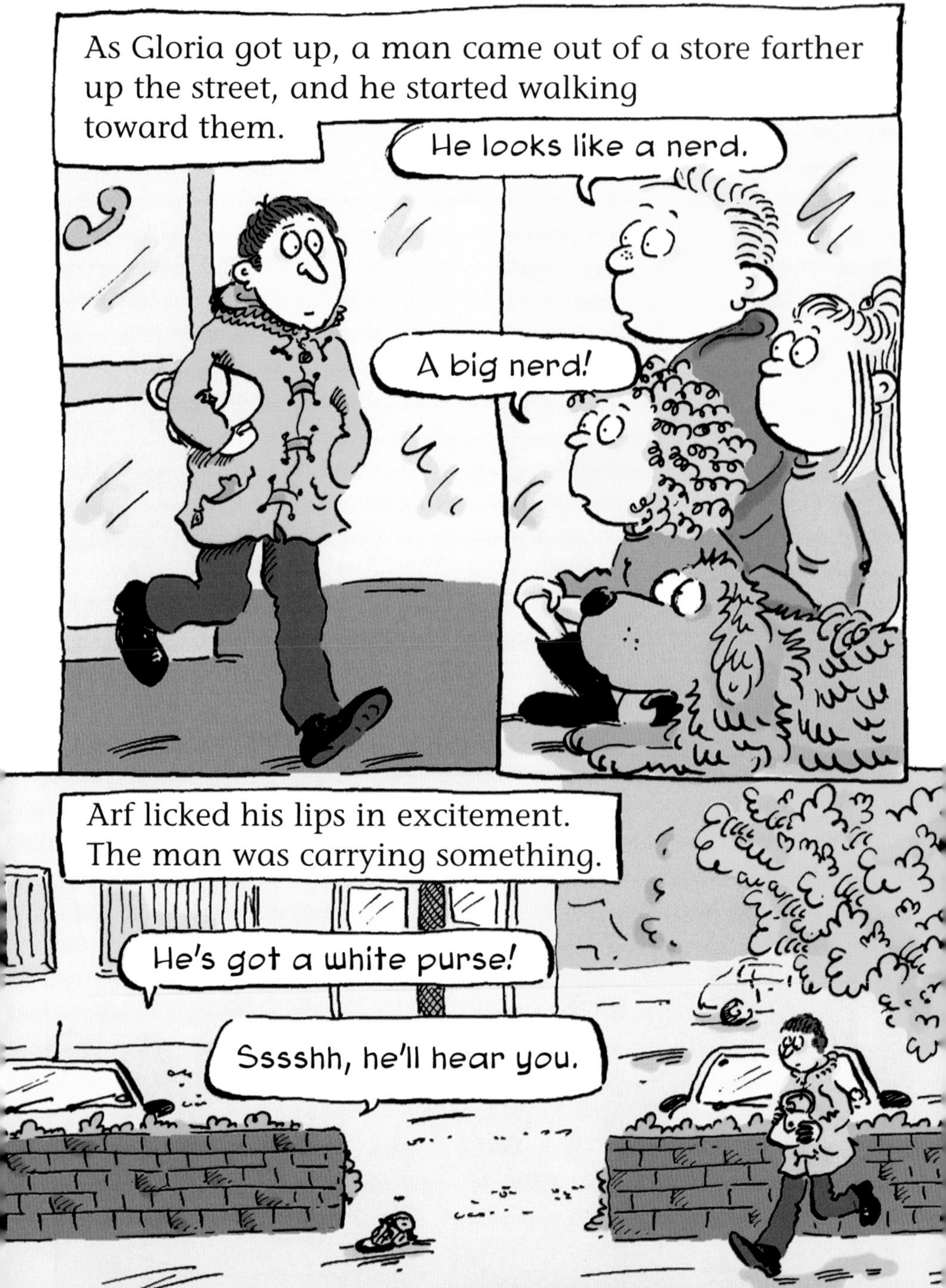
As Gloria got up, a man came out of a store farther up the street, and he started walking toward them.
He looks like a nerd.
A big nerd!
Arf licked his lips in excitement. The man was carrying something.
He's got a white purse!
Sssshh, he'll hear you.

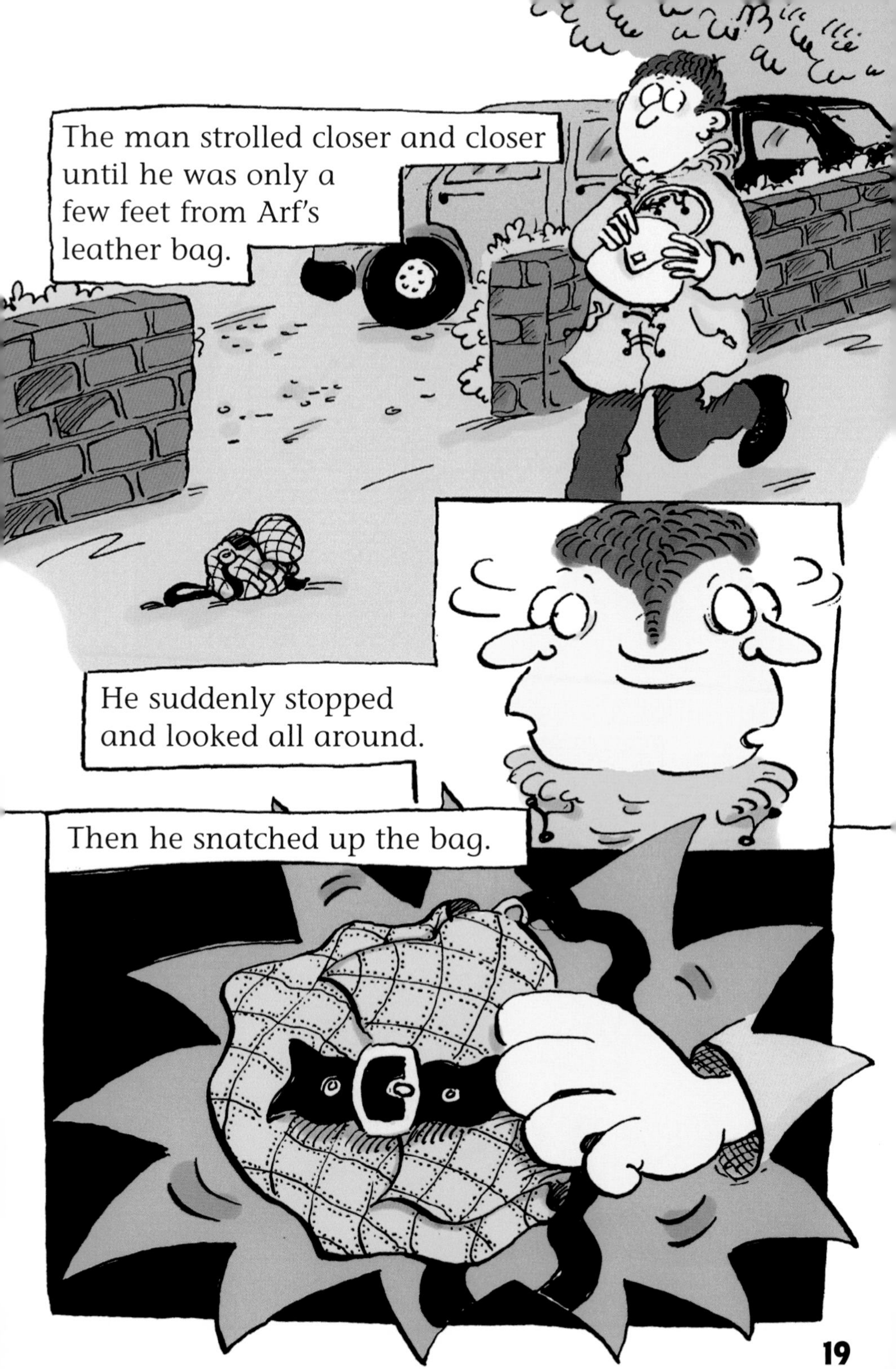
The man strolled closer and closer until he was only a few feet from Arf's leather bag.
He suddenly stopped and looked all around.
Then he snatched up the bag.

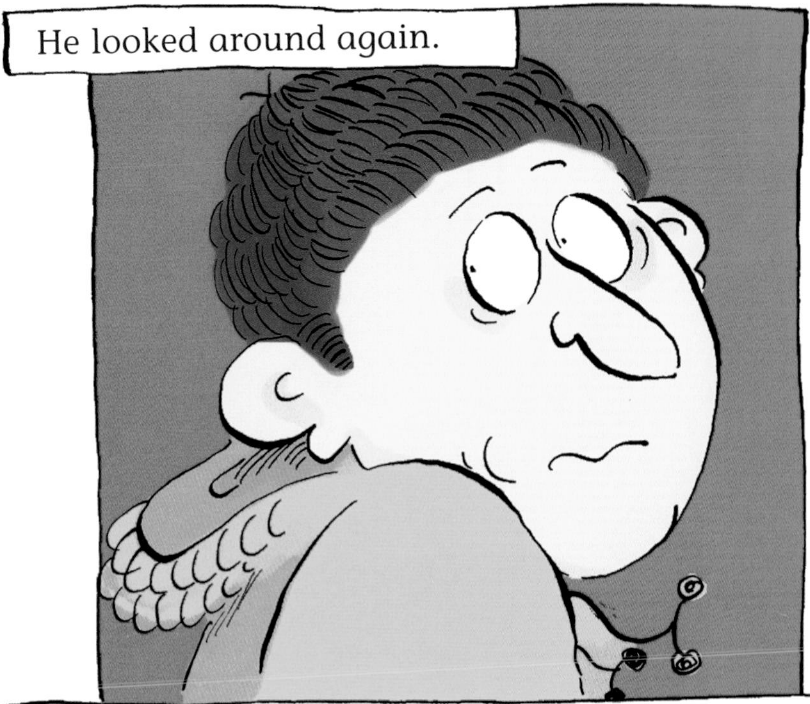
He looked around again.

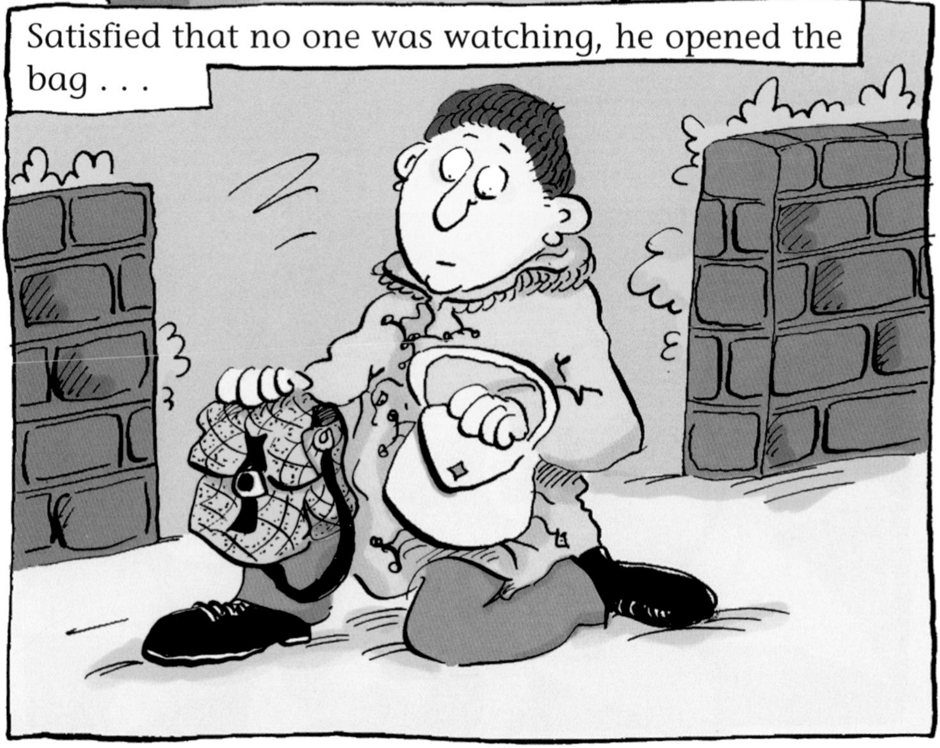
Satisfied that no one was watching, he opened the bag . . .

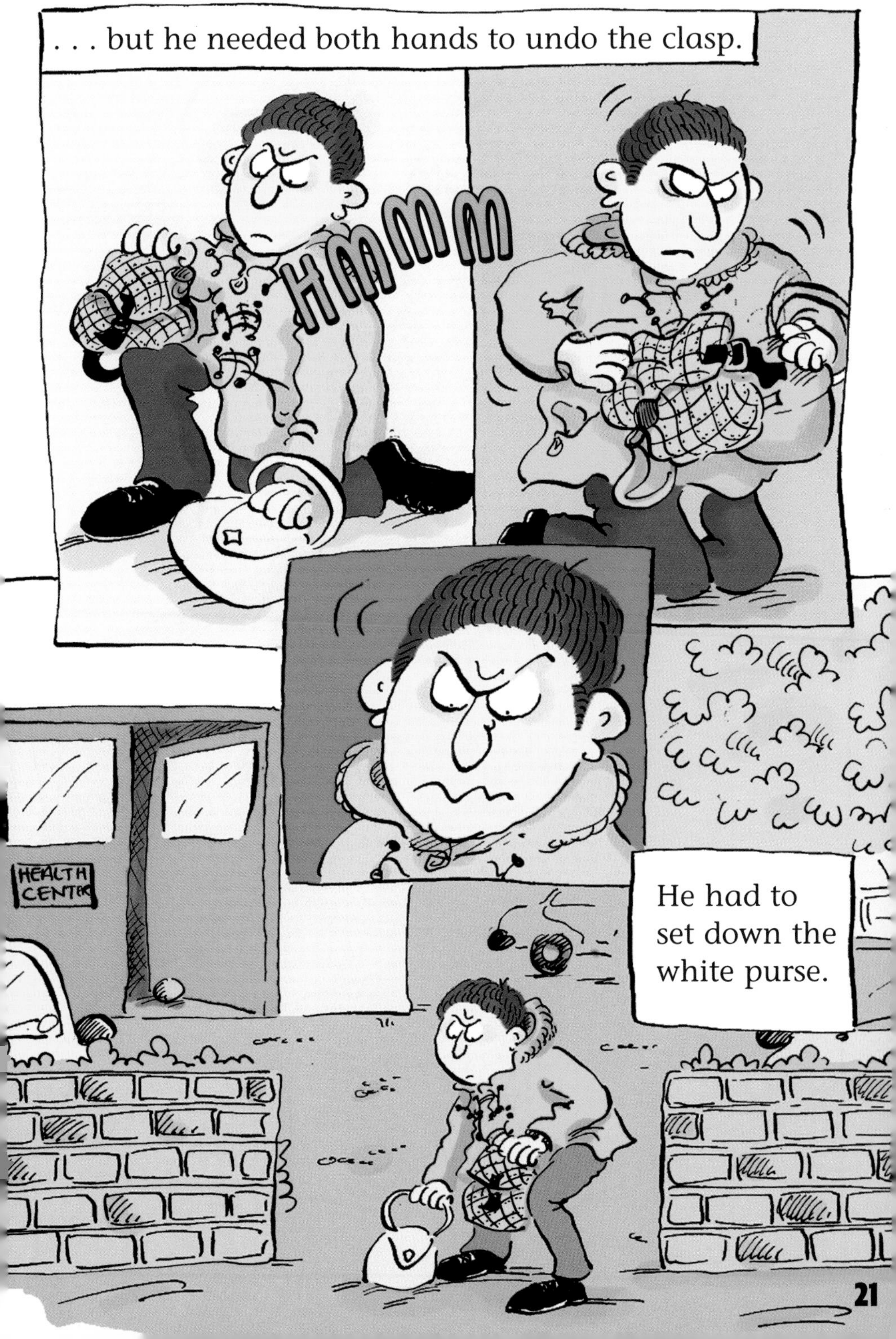
. . . but he needed both hands to undo the clasp.
HMMM
HEALTH CENTER
He had to set down the white purse.

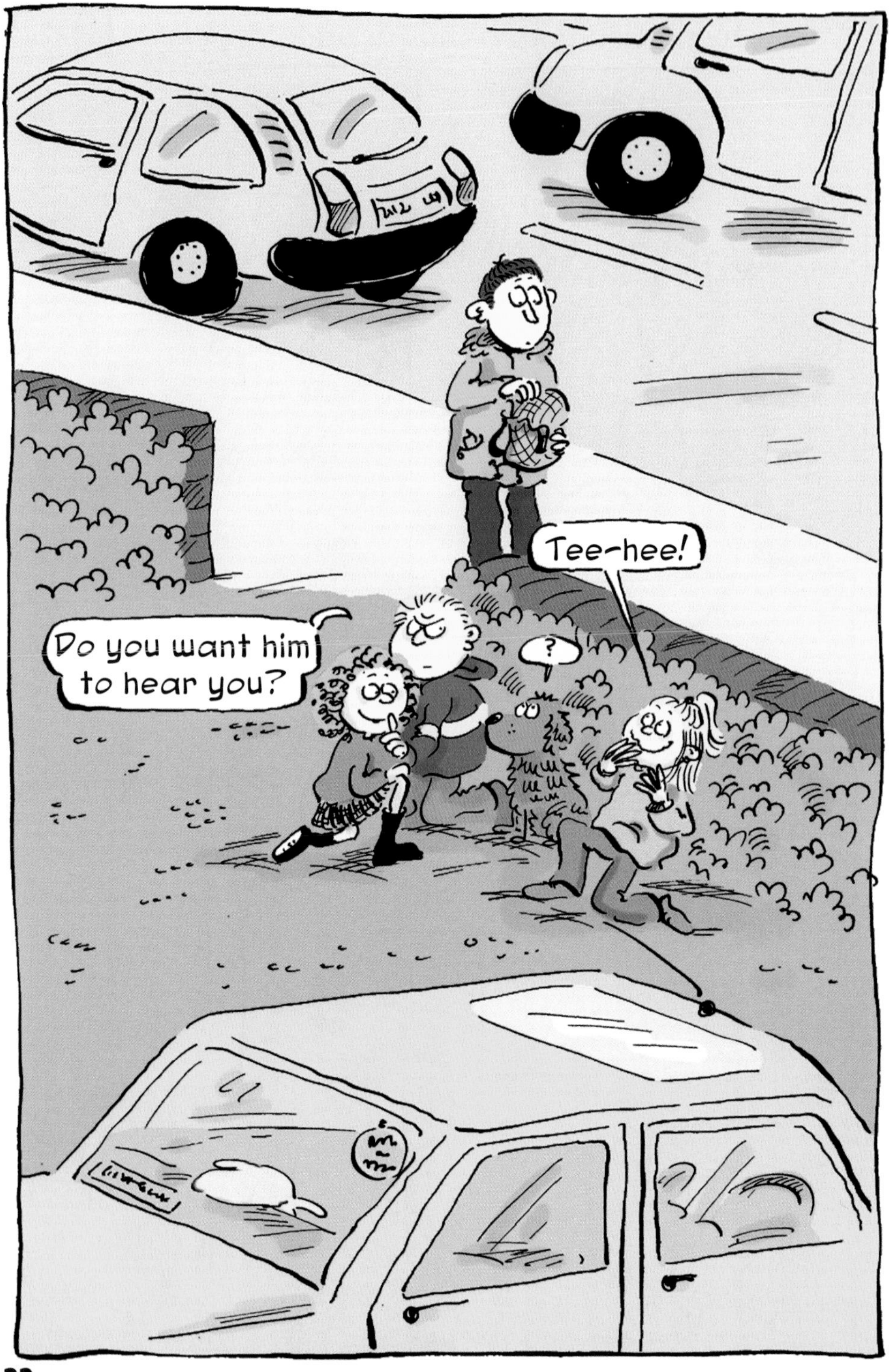
Tee-hee!
Do you want him to hear you?
?

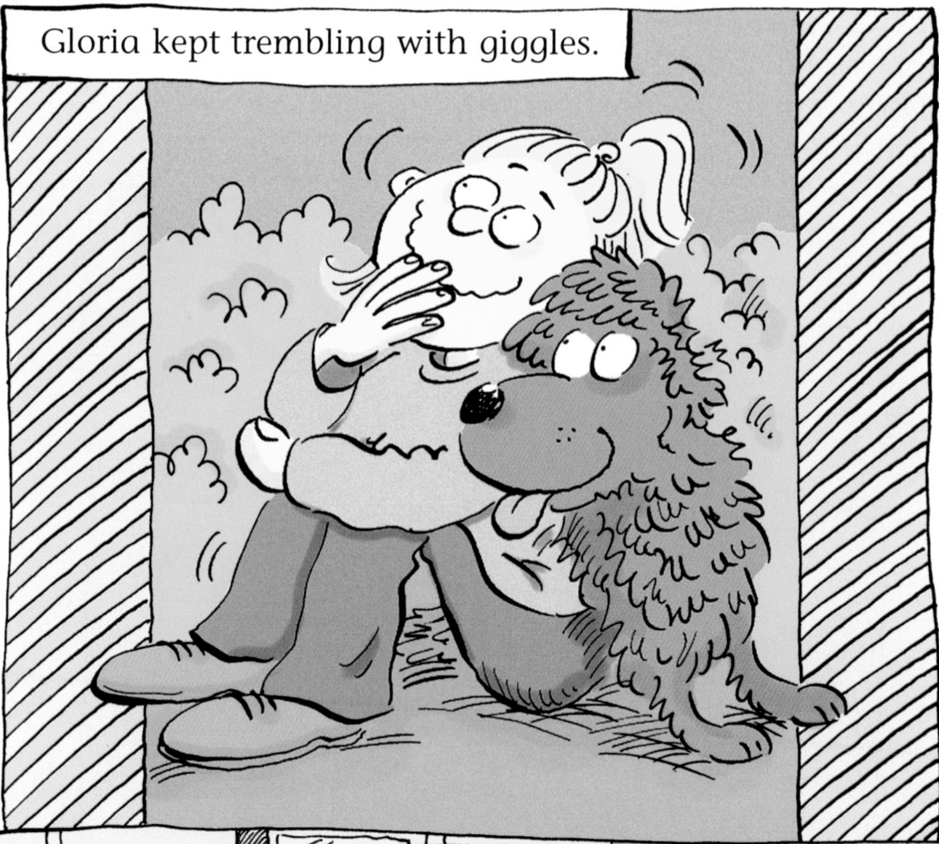
Gloria kept trembling with giggles.

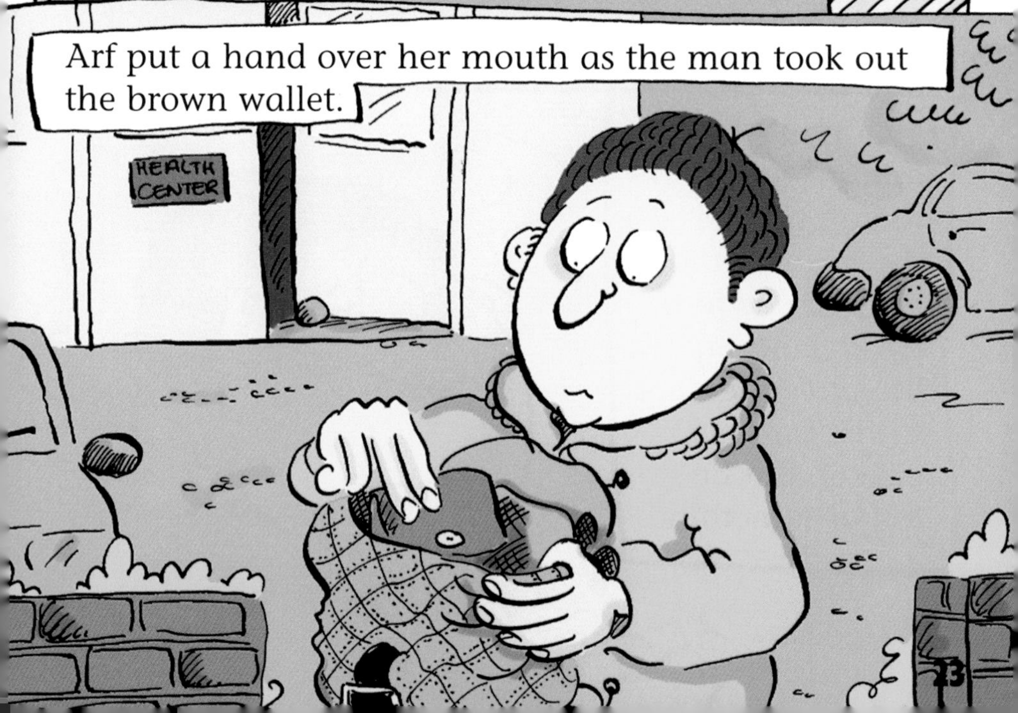
Arf put a hand over her mouth as the man took out the brown wallet.
HEALTH CENTER

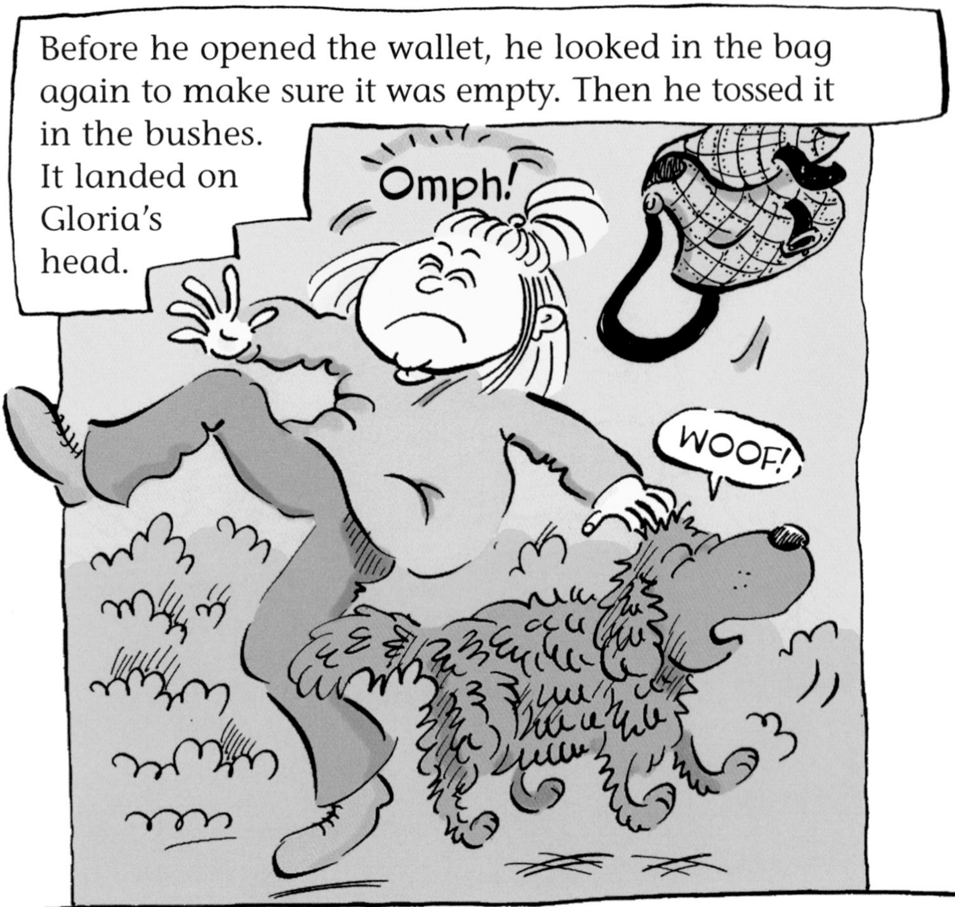

Before he opened the wallet, he looked in the bag again to make sure it was empty. Then he tossed it in the bushes. It landed on Gloria's head.
Omph!
WOOF!

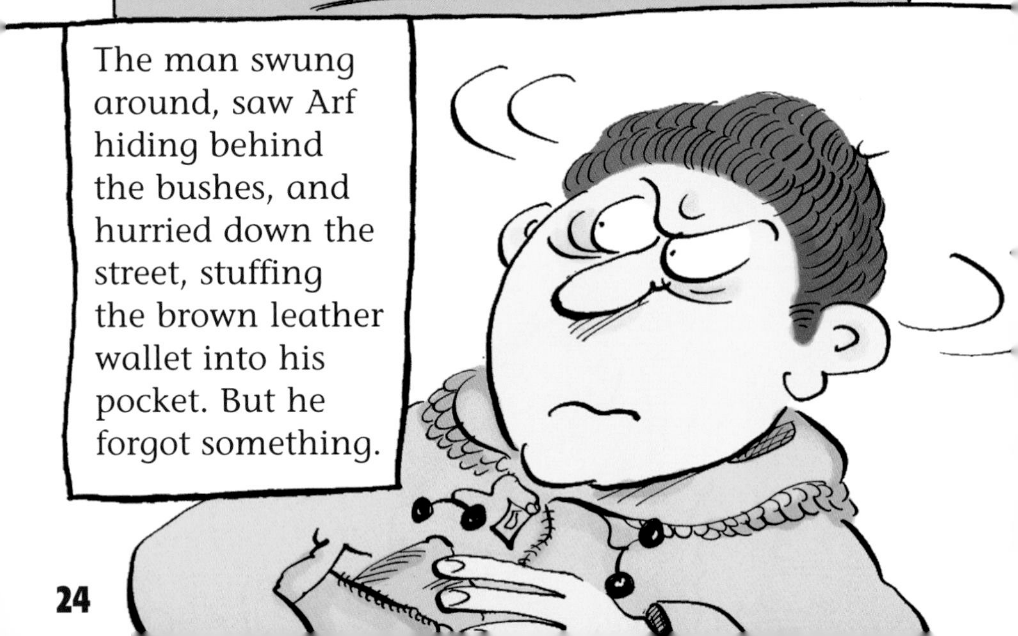

The man swung around, saw Arf hiding behind the bushes, and hurried down the street, stuffing the brown leather wallet into his pocket. But he forgot something.

CHAPTER THREE

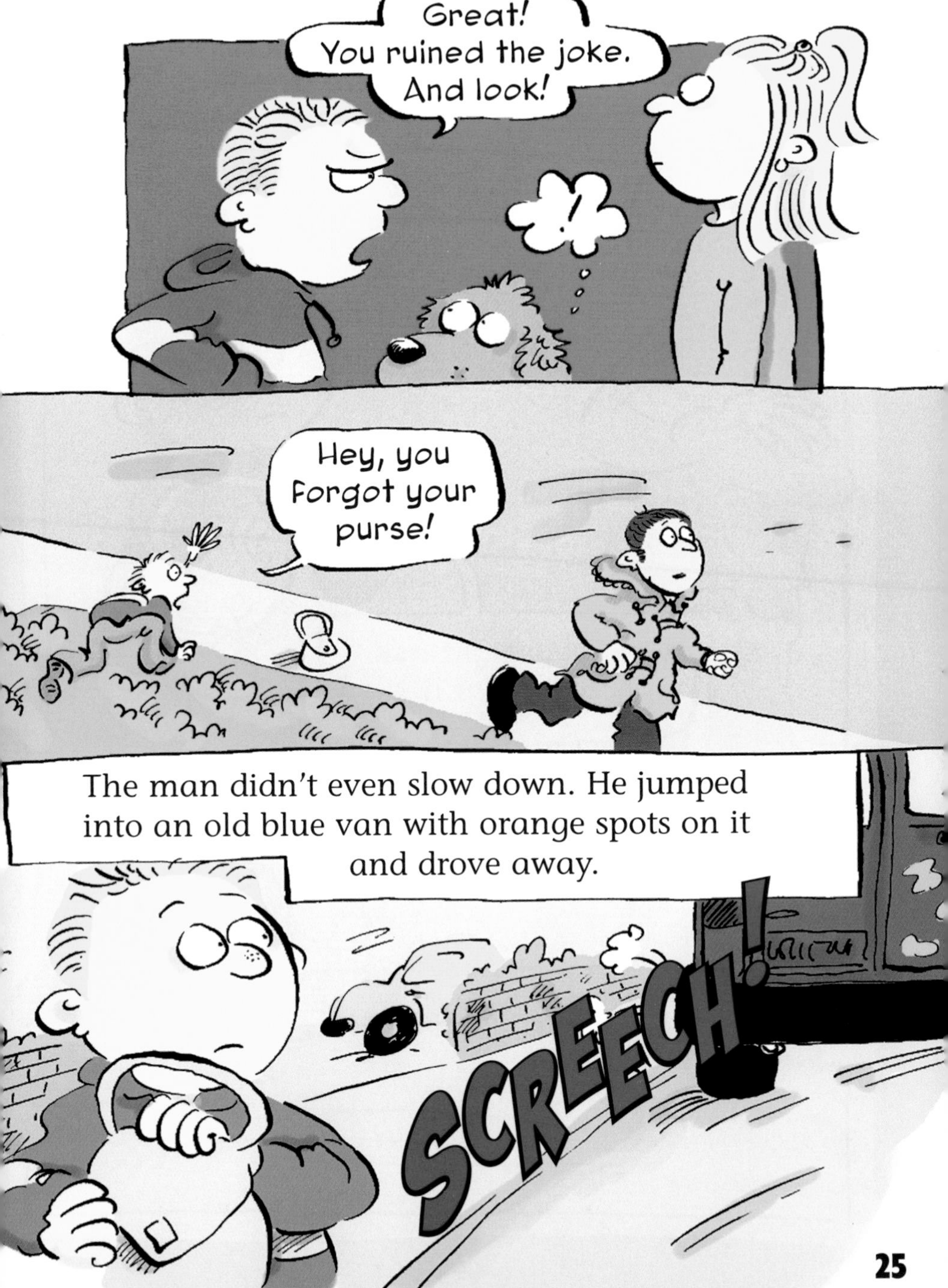

Great! You ruined the joke. And look!
!
Hey, you forgot your purse!
The man didn't even slow down. He jumped into an old blue van with orange spots on it and drove away.
SCREECH!

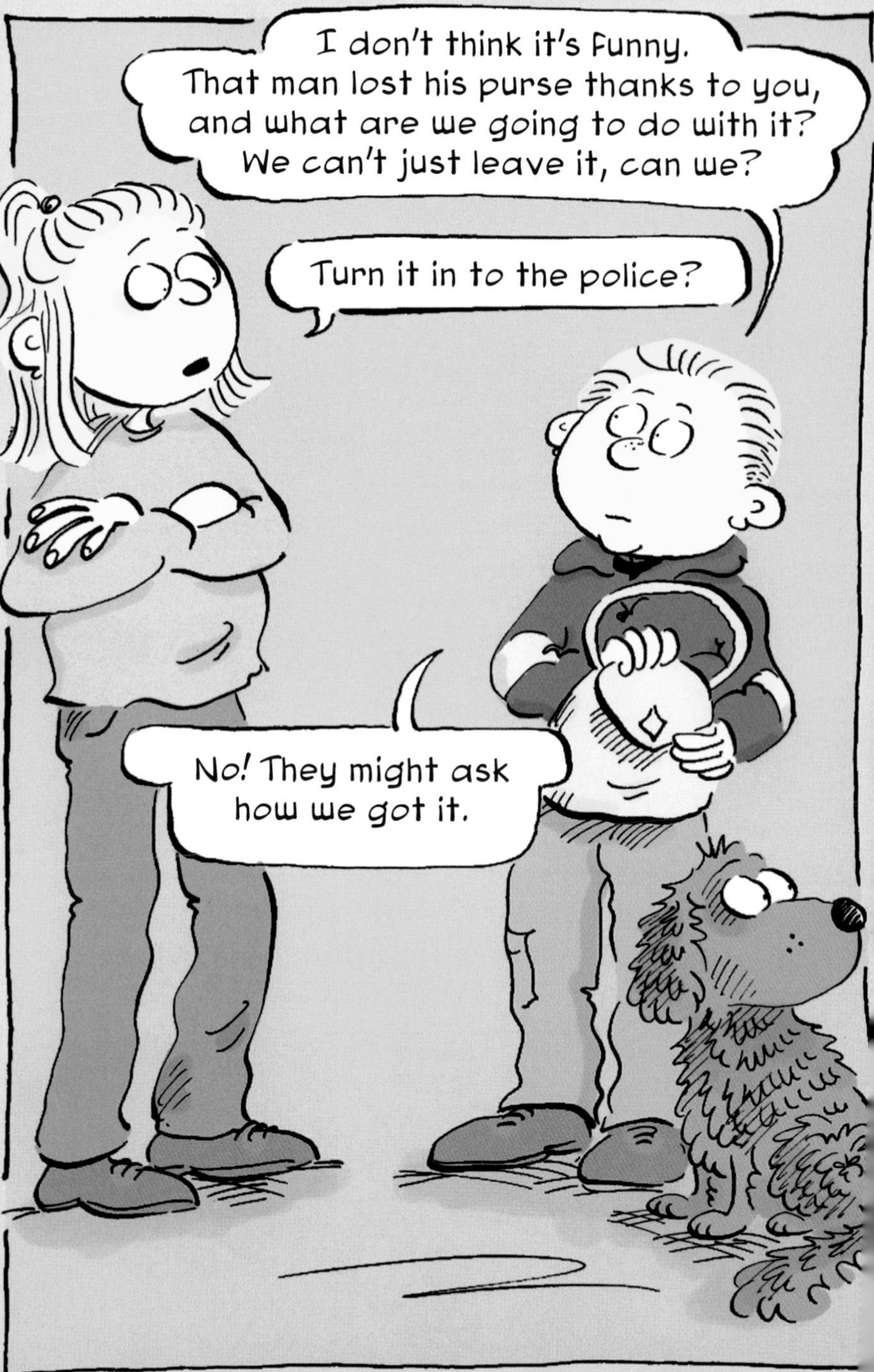
I don't think it's funny. That man lost his purse thanks to you, and what are we going to do with it? We can't just leave it, can we?
Turn it in to the police?
No! They might ask how we got it.

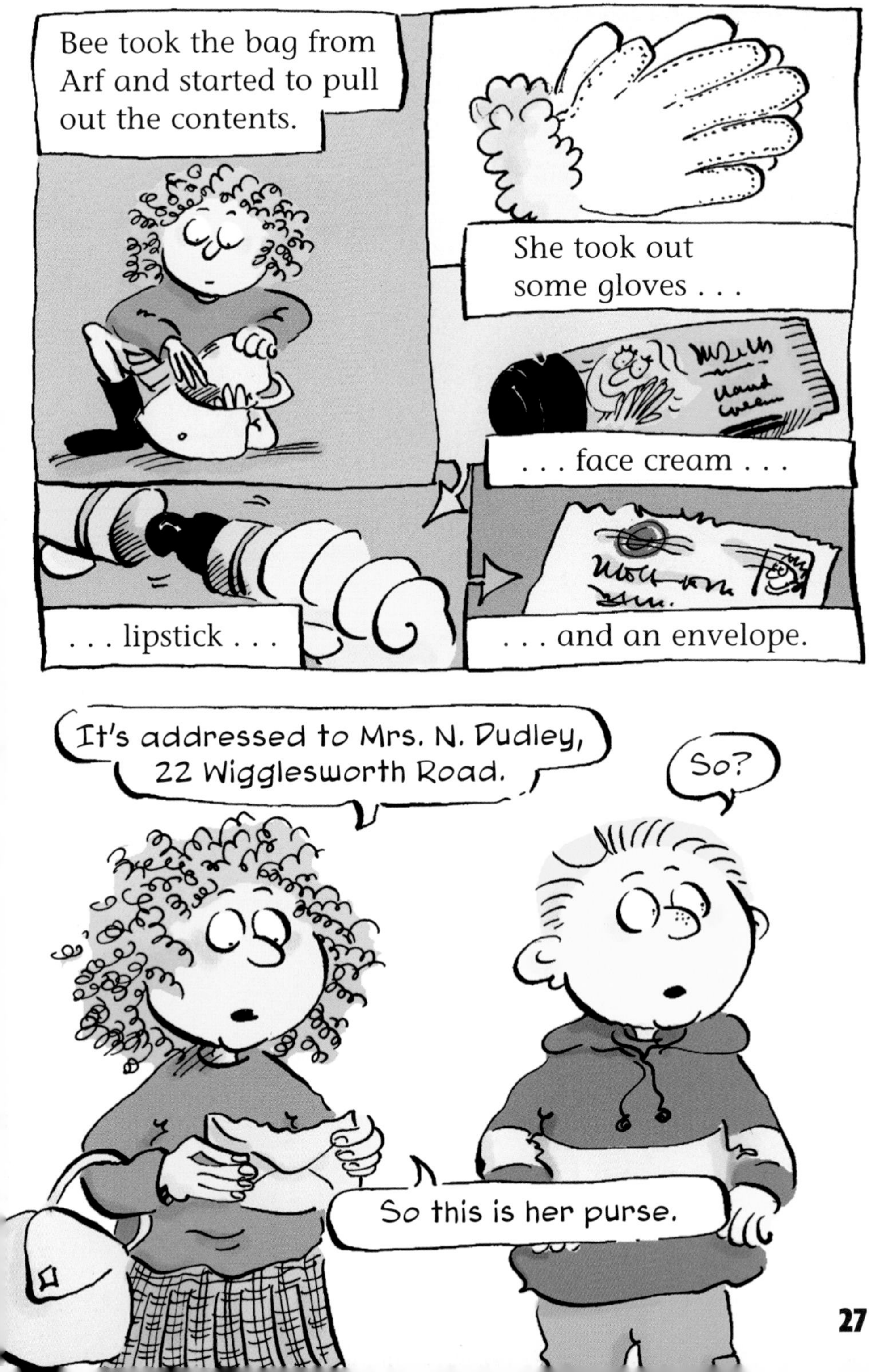
Bee took the bag from Arf and started to pull out the contents.
She took out some gloves . . .
. . . face cream . . .
. . . lipstick . . .
. . . and an envelope.
It's addressed to Mrs. N. Dudley, 22 Wigglesworth Road.
So?
So this is her purse.

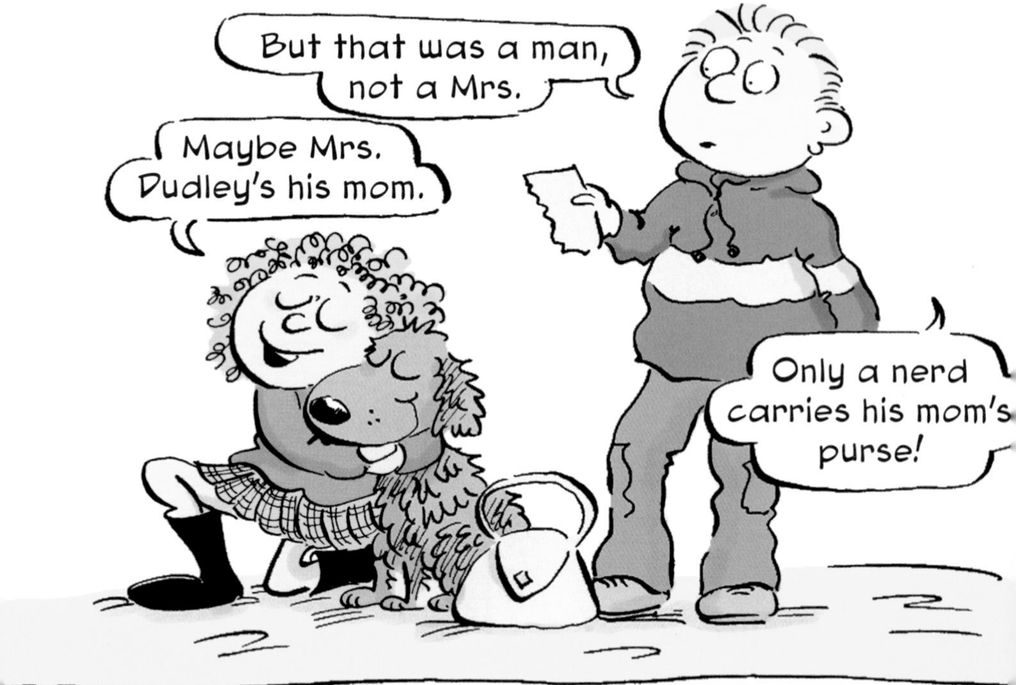
But that was a man, not a Mrs.
Maybe Mrs. Dudley's his mom.
Only a nerd carries his mom's purse!

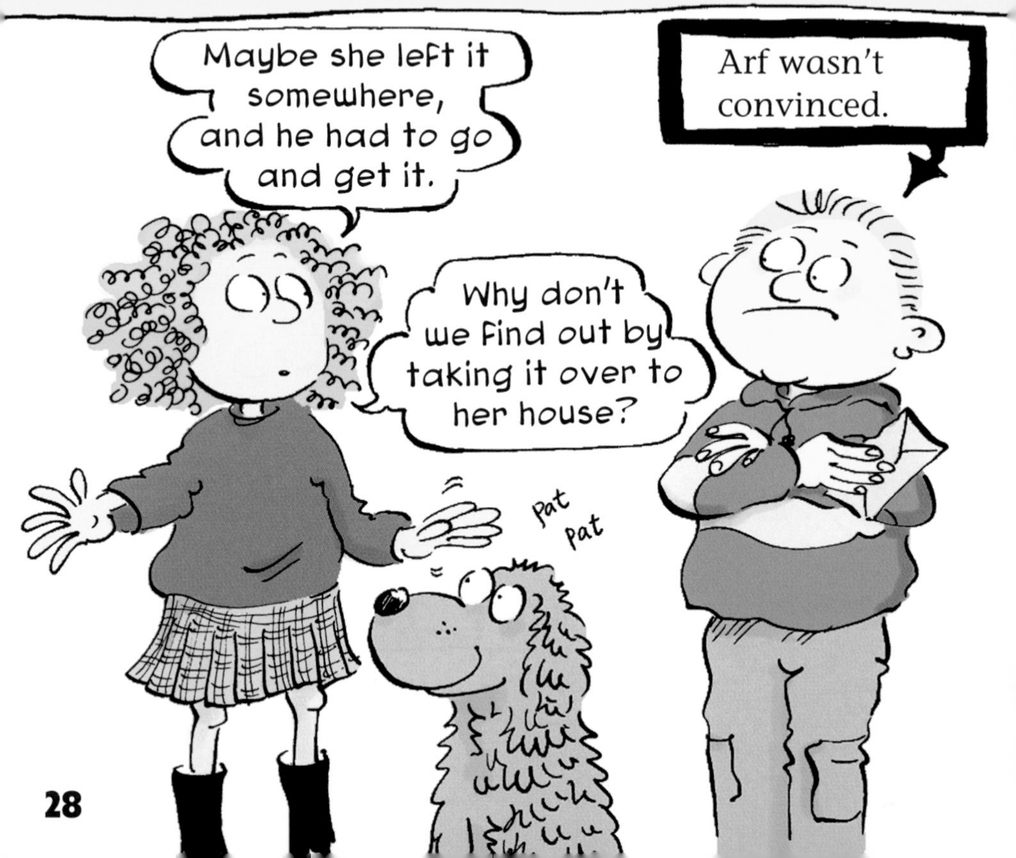
Maybe she left it somewhere, and he had to go and get it.
Arf wasn't convinced.
Why don't we find out by taking it over to her house?
pat pat

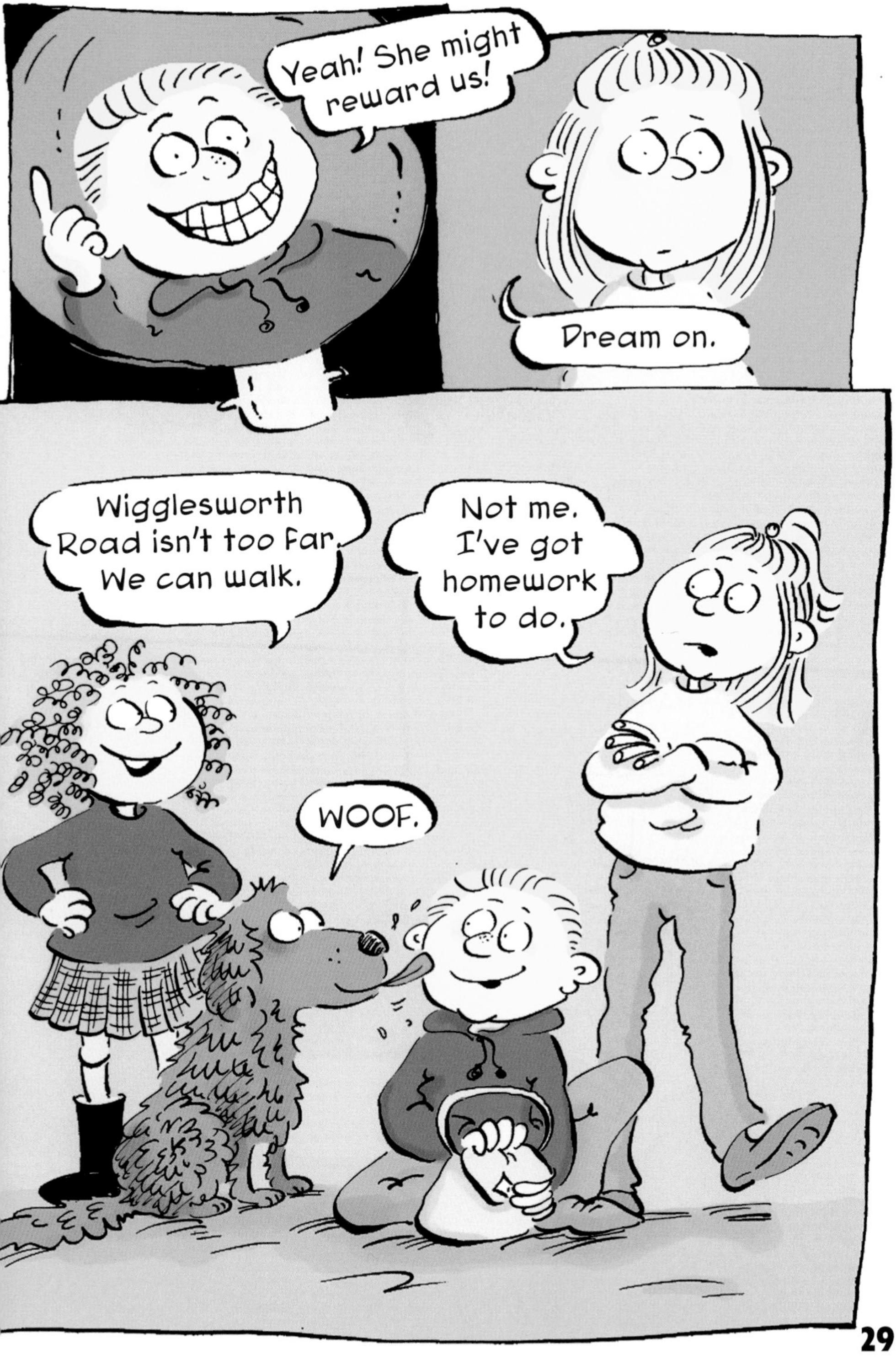
Yeah! She might reward us!
Dream on.
Wigglesworth Road isn't too far. We can walk.
Not me. I've got homework to do.
WOOF.

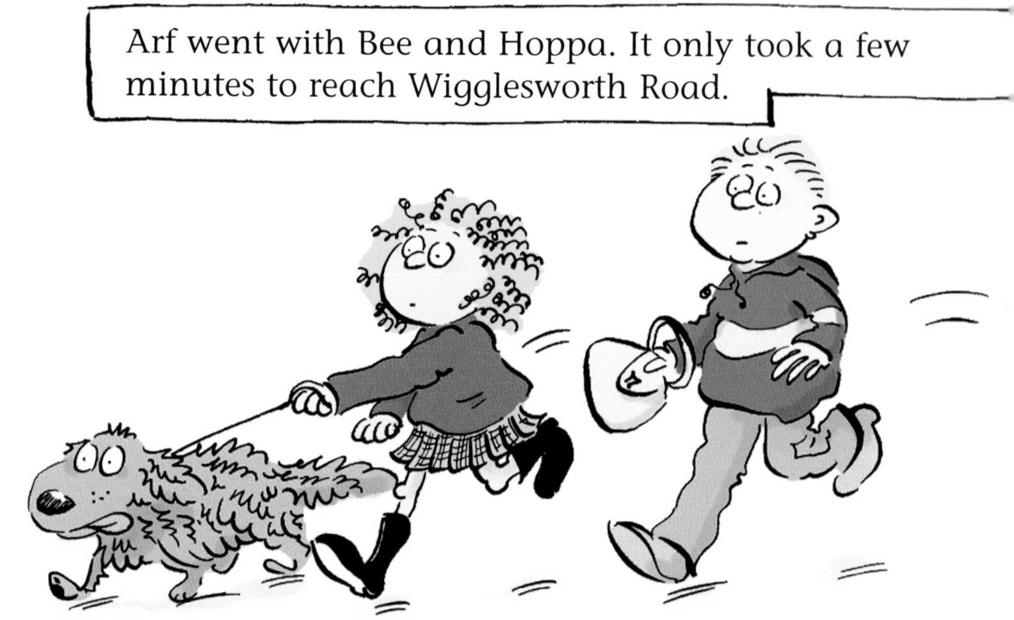
Arf went with Bee and Hoppa. It only took a few minutes to reach Wigglesworth Road.

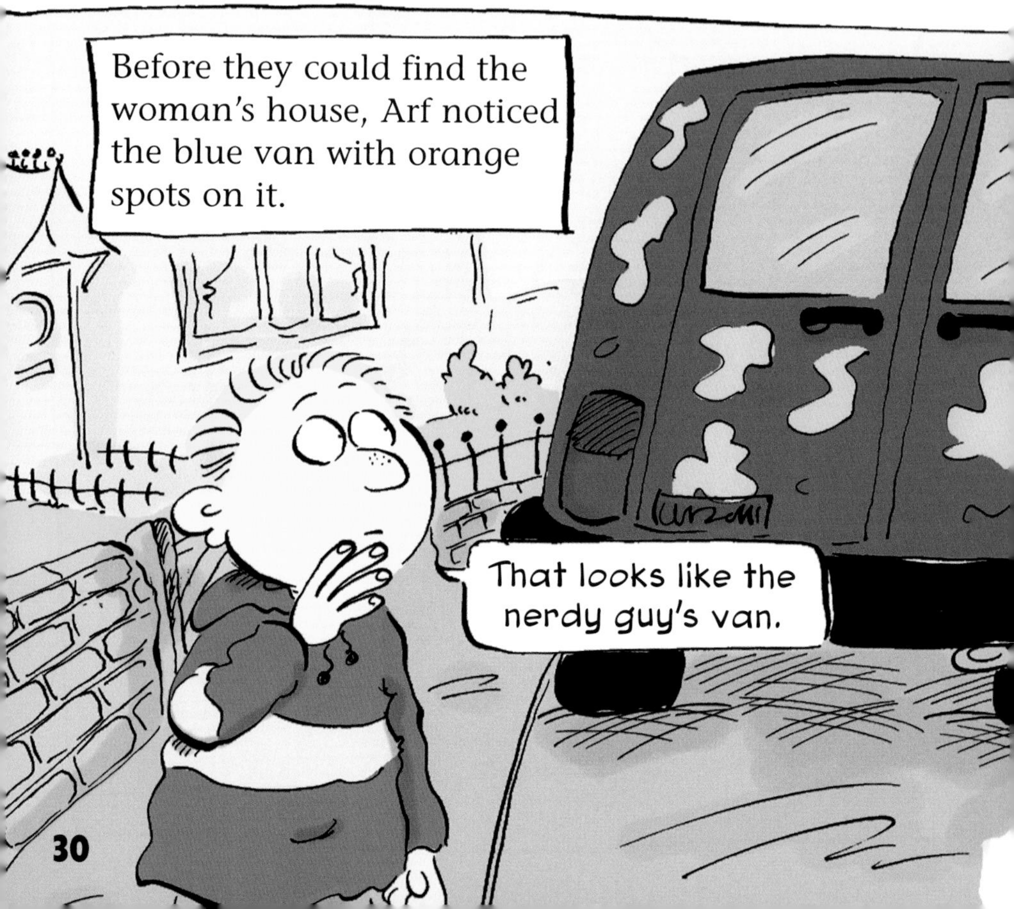
Before they could find the woman's house, Arf noticed the blue van with orange spots on it.
That looks like the nerdy guy's van.

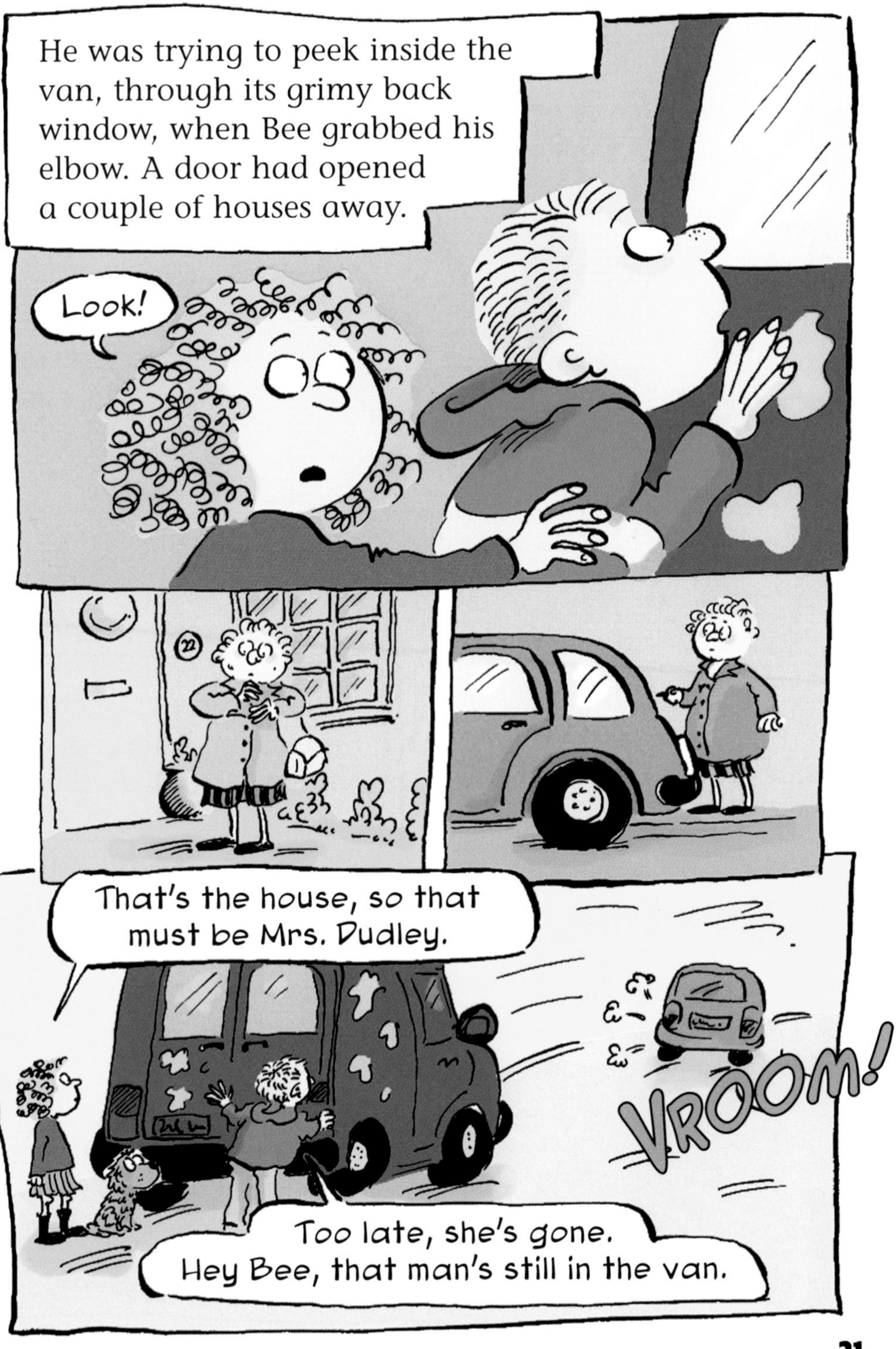

He was trying to peek inside the van, through its grimy back window, when Bee grabbed his elbow. A door had opened a couple of houses away.
Look!
That's the house, so that must be Mrs. Dudley.
VROOM!
Too late, she's gone. Hey Bee, that man's still in the van.

CHAPTER FOUR

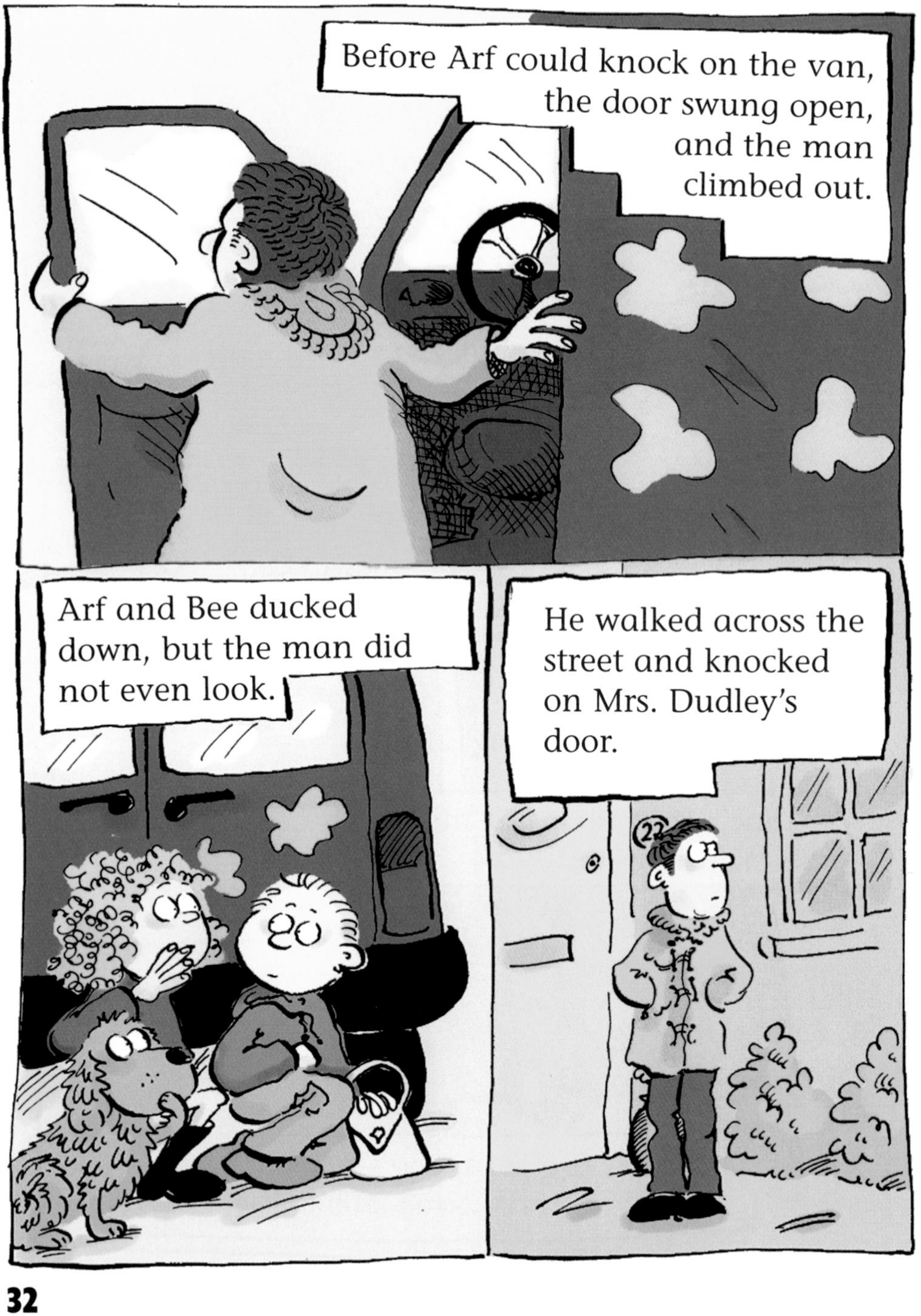
Before Arf could knock on the van, the door swung open, and the man climbed out.
Arf and Bee ducked down, but the man did not even look.
He walked across the street and knocked on Mrs. Dudley's door.
22

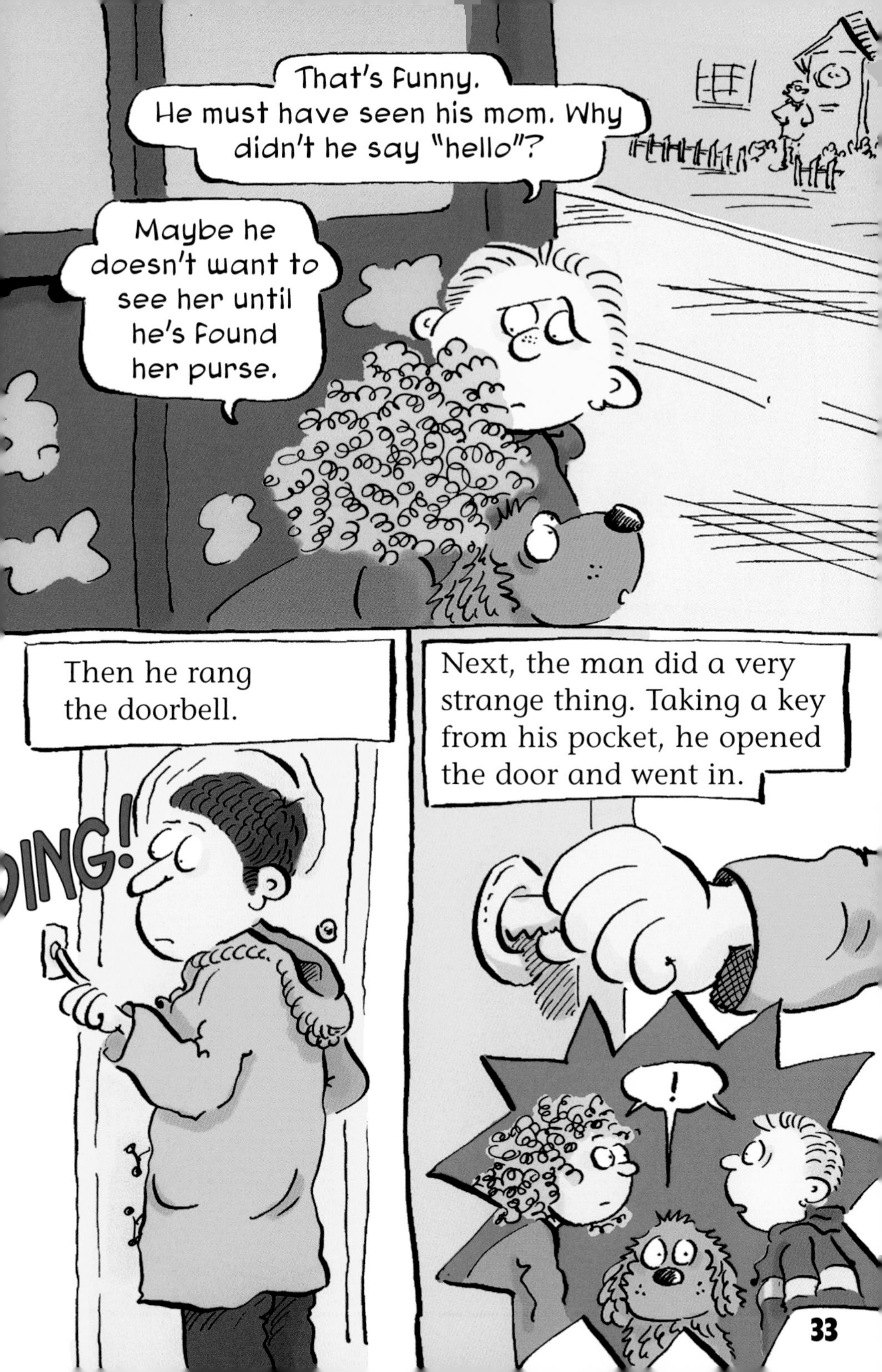
That's funny.
He must have seen his mom. Why didn't he say "hello"?
Maybe he doesn't want to see her until he's found her purse.
Then he rang the doorbell.
DING!
Next, the man did a very strange thing. Taking a key from his pocket, he opened the door and went in.
!

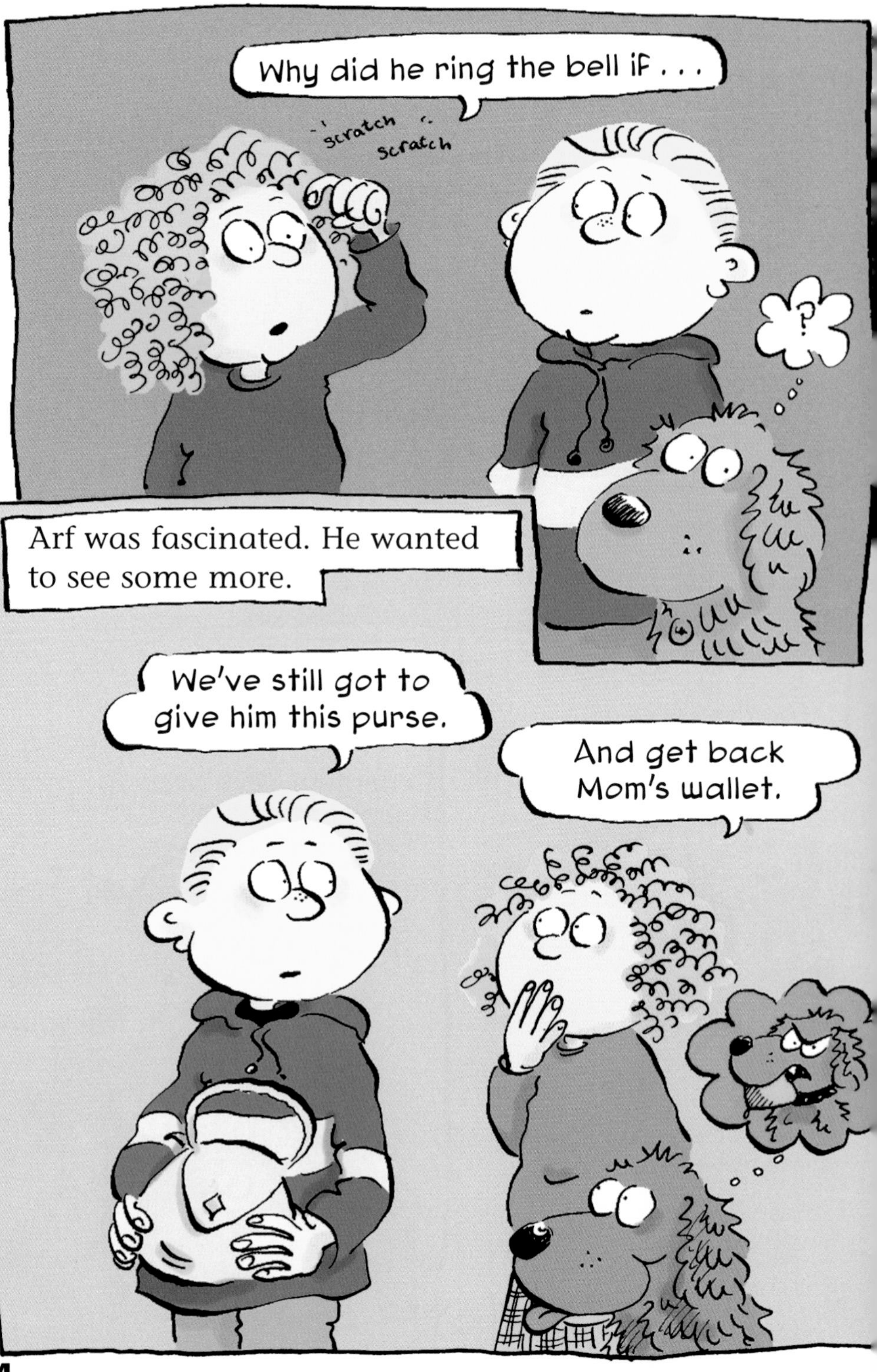
Why did he ring the bell if . . .
scratch
scratch
?
Arf was fascinated. He wanted to see some more.
We've still got to give him this purse.
And get back Mom's wallet.

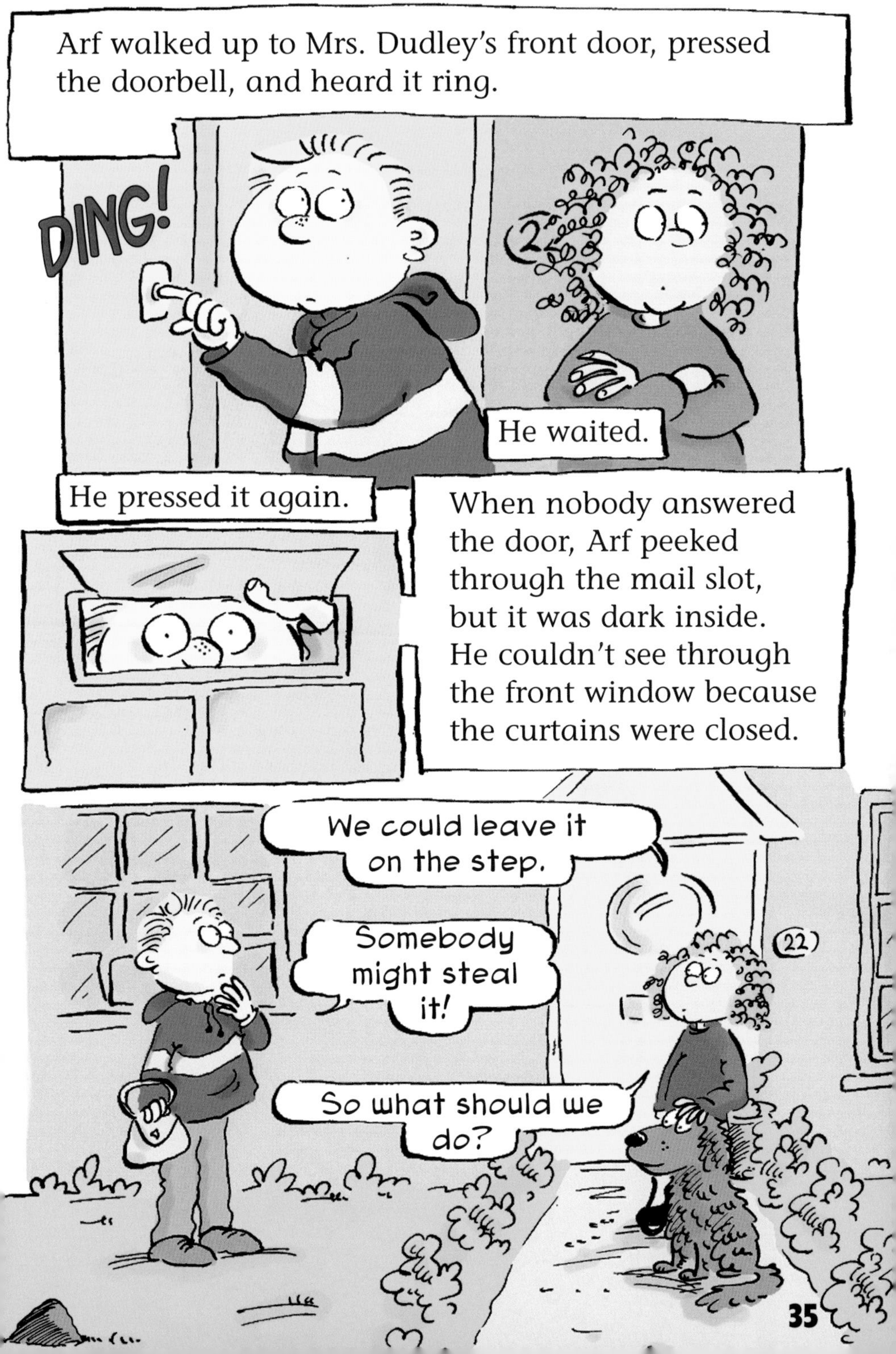
Arf walked up to Mrs. Dudley's front door, pressed the doorbell, and heard it ring.
DING!
He waited.
He pressed it again.
When nobody answered the door, Arf peeked through the mail slot, but it was dark inside. He couldn't see through the front window because the curtains were closed.
We could leave it on the step.
Somebody might steal it!
So what should we do?

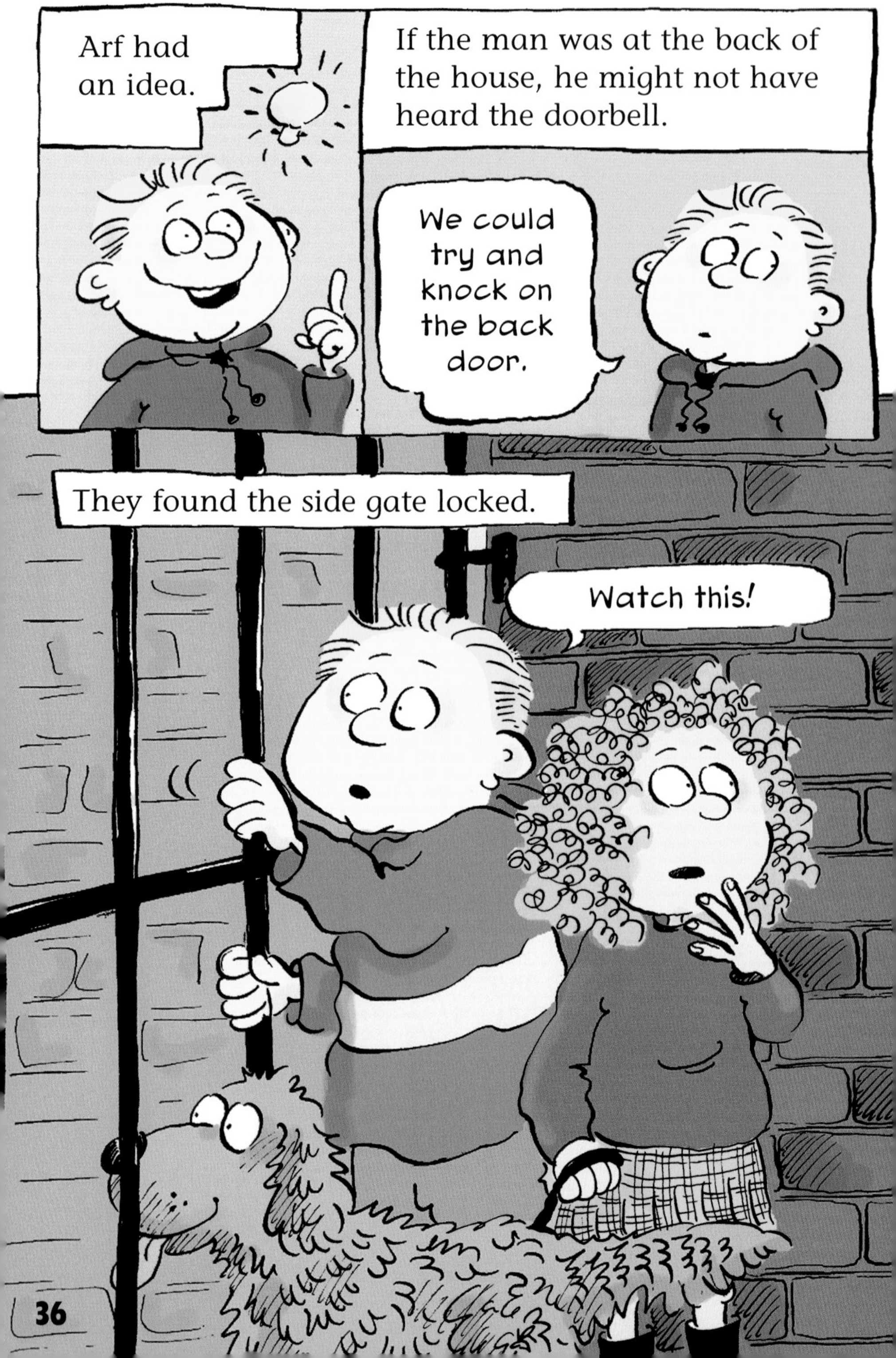

Arf had an idea.
If the man was at the back of the house, he might not have heard the doorbell.
We could try and knock on the back door.
They found the side gate locked.
Watch this!

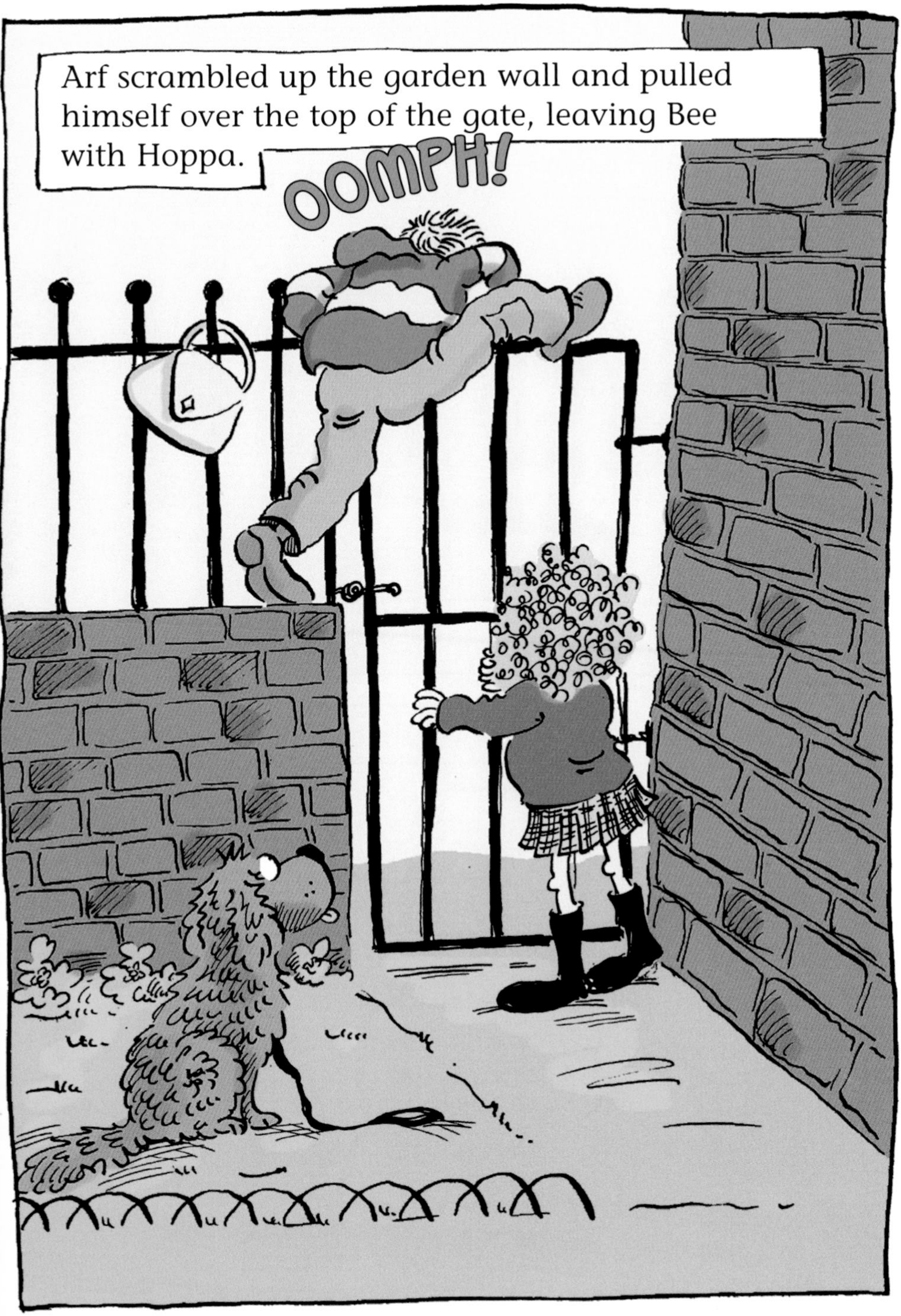
Arf scrambled up the garden wall and pulled himself over the top of the gate, leaving Bee with Hoppa.
OOMPH!

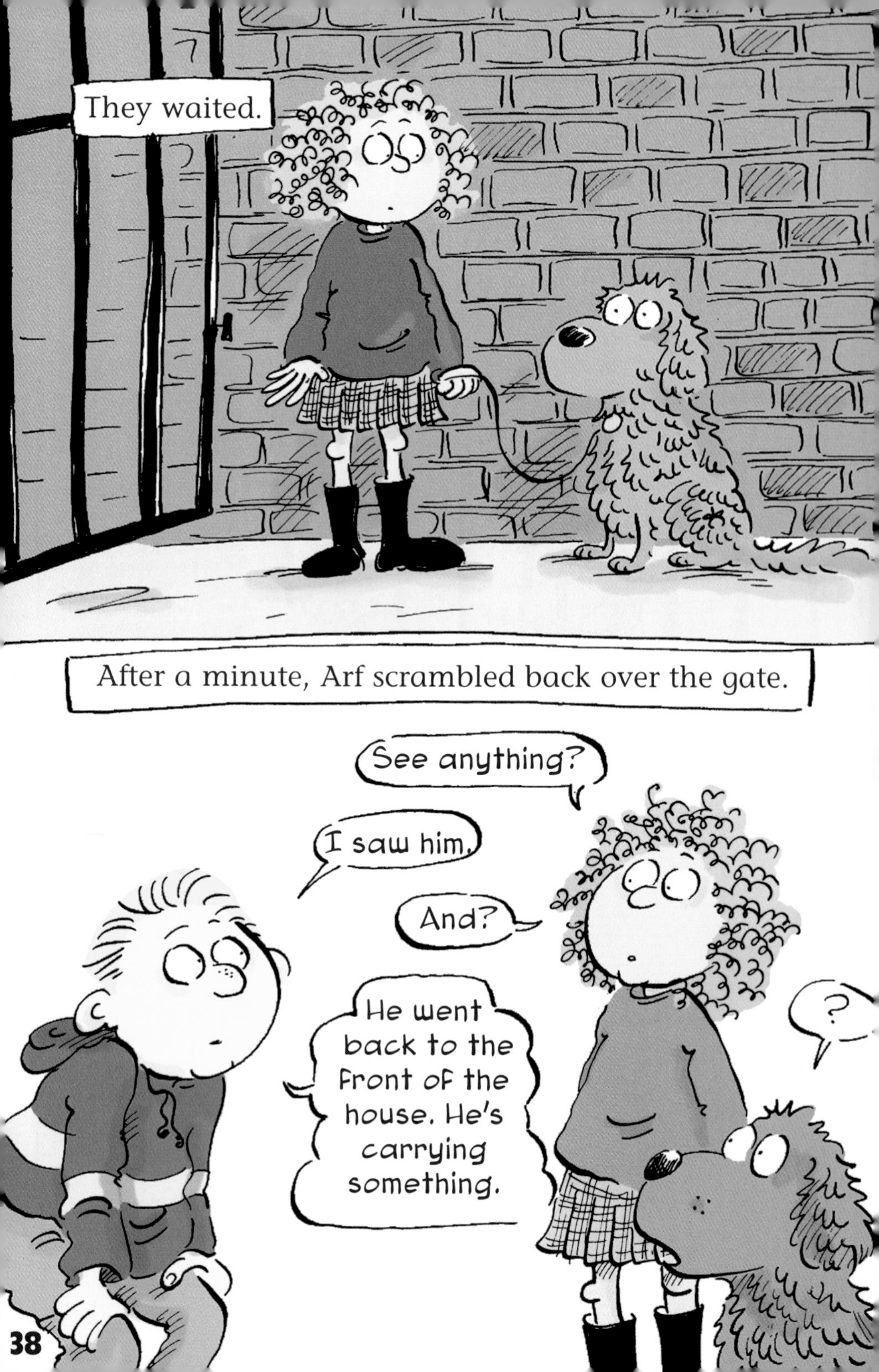
They waited.
After a minute, Arf scrambled back over the gate.
See anything?
I saw him.
And?
He went back to the front of the house. He's carrying something.
?

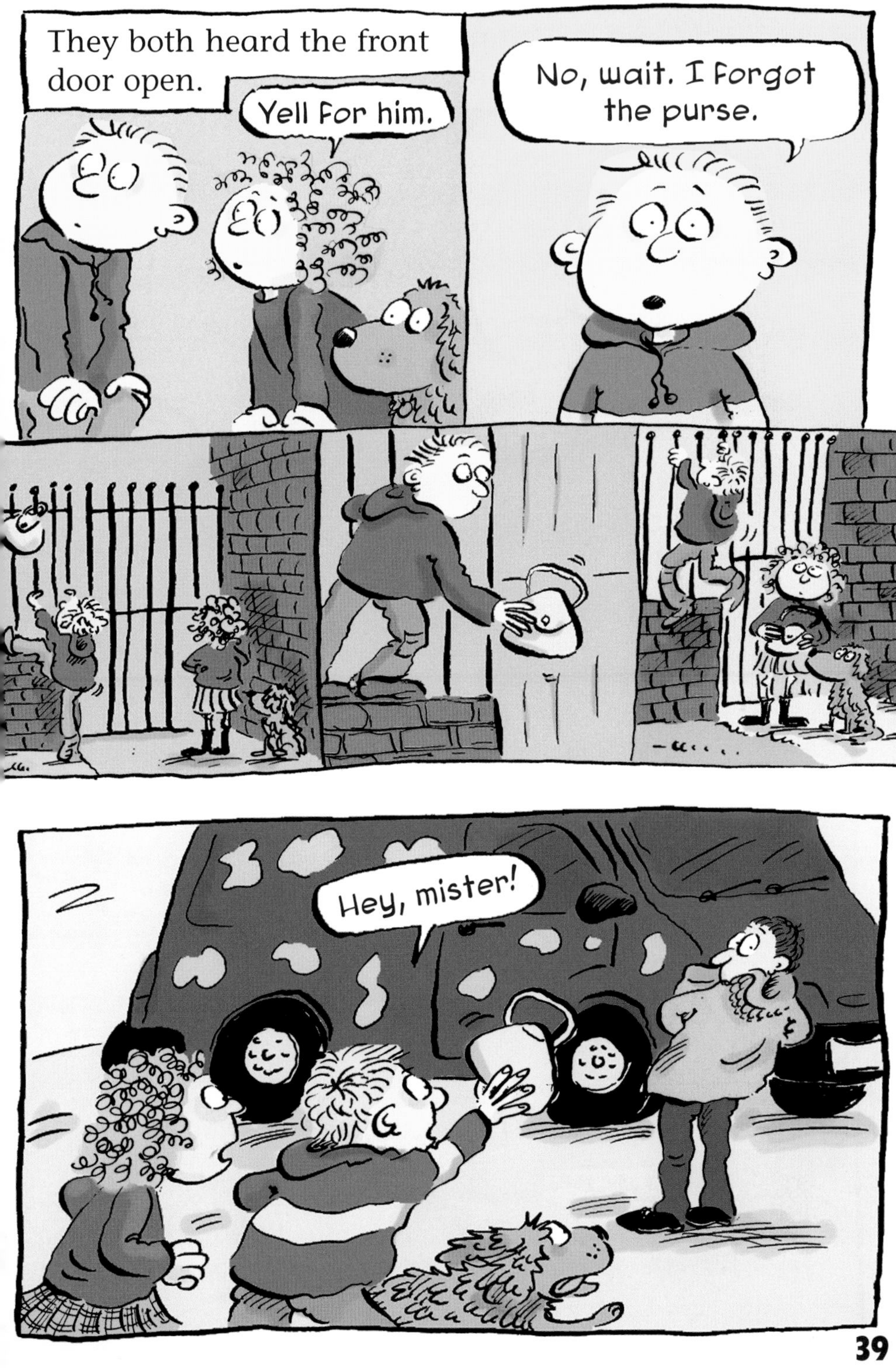
They both heard the front door open.
Yell for him.
No, wait. I forgot the purse.
Hey, mister!

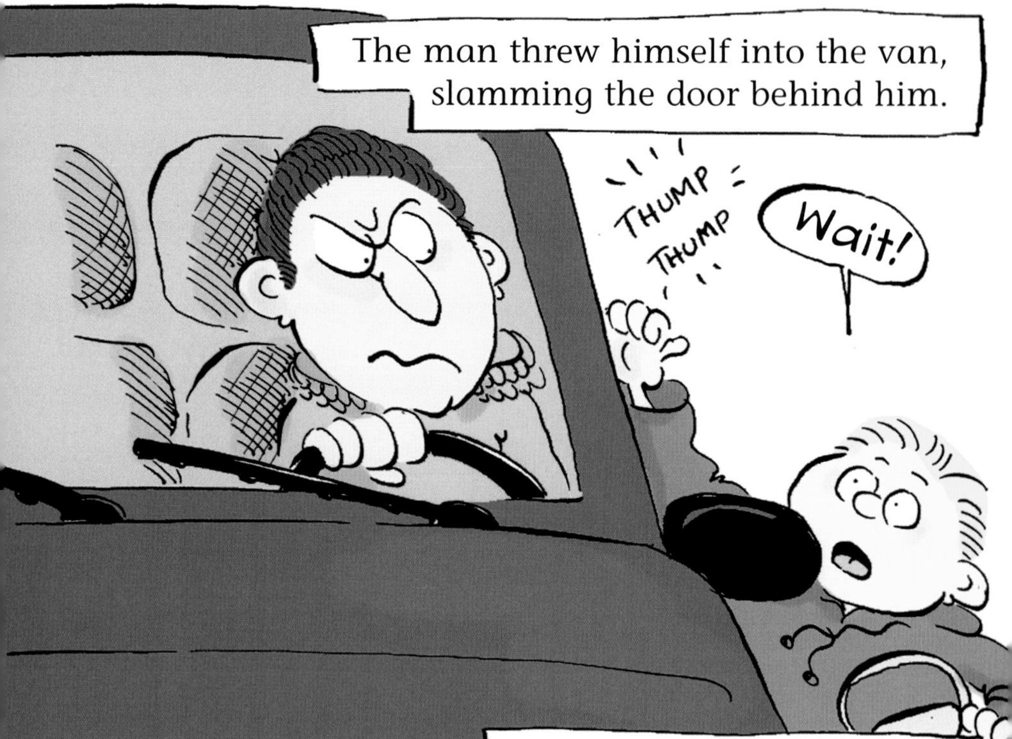
The man threw himself into the van, slamming the door behind him.
THUMP THUMP
Wait!

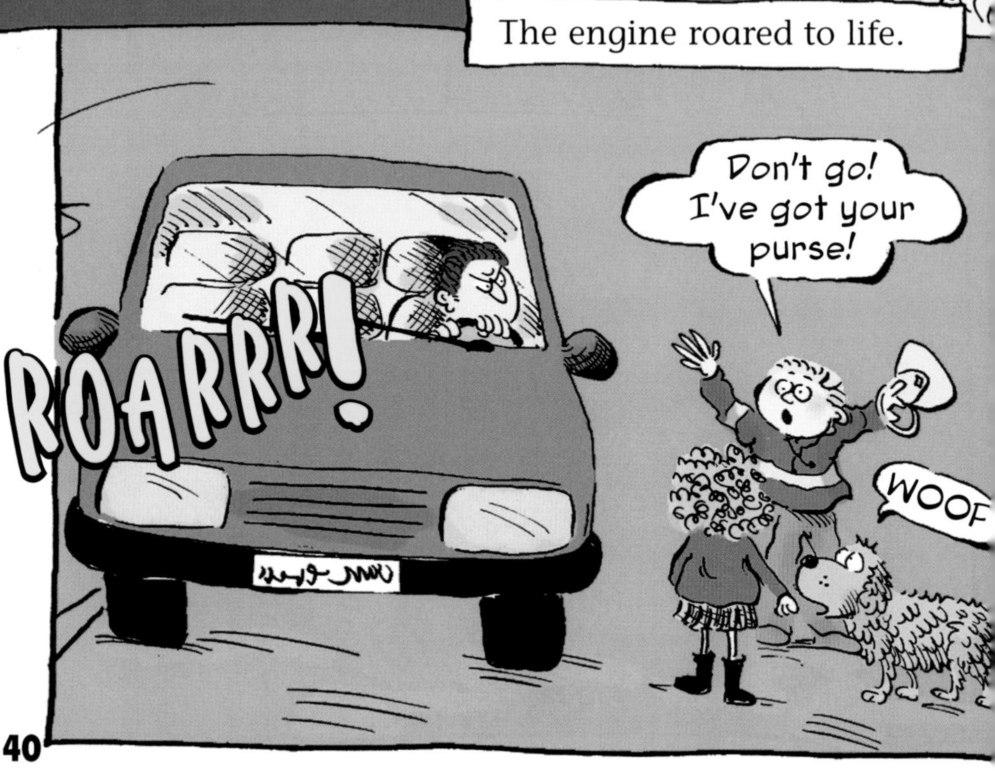
The engine roared to life.
Don't go! I've got your purse!
ROARRR!
WOOF

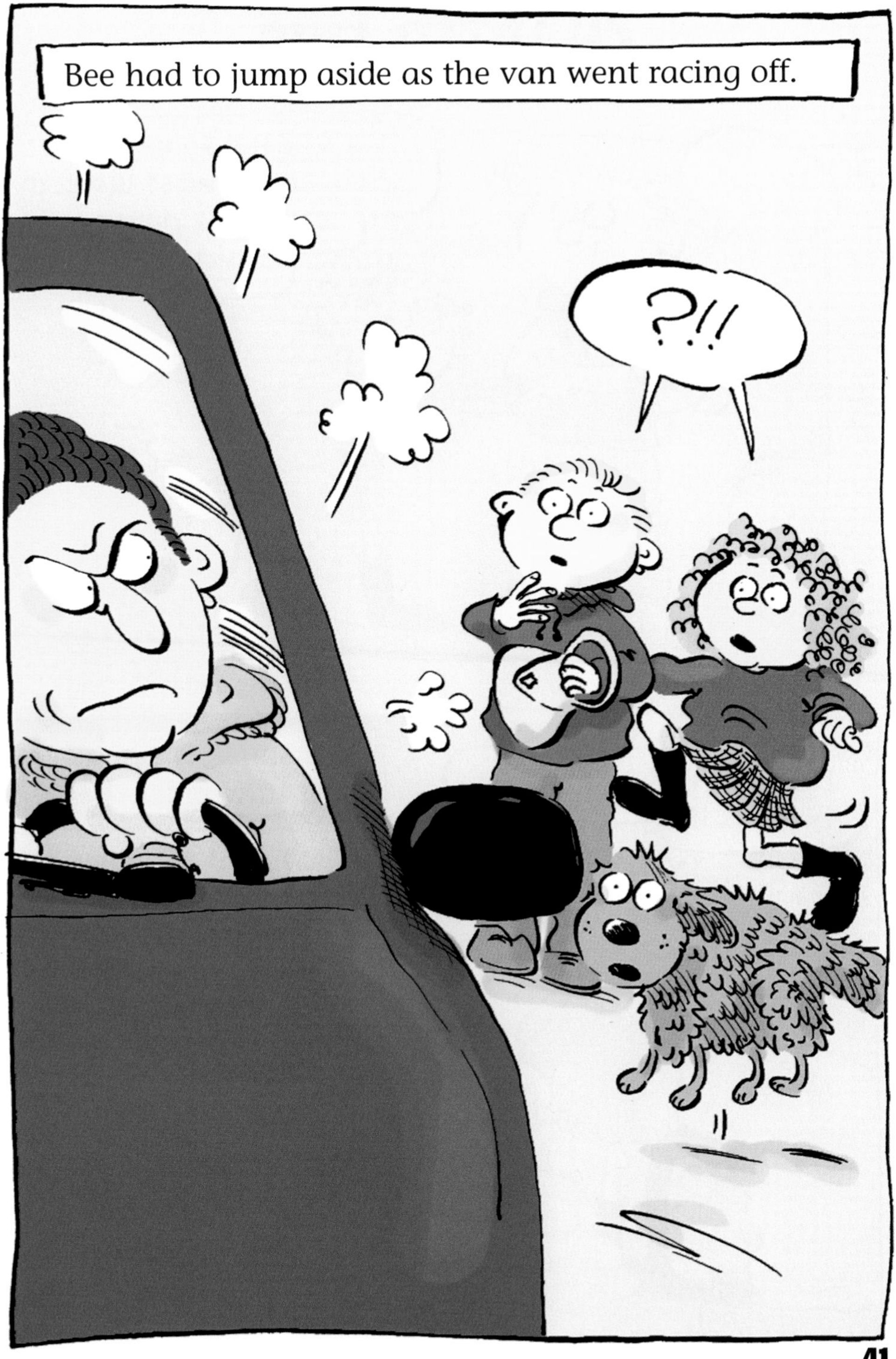
Bee had to jump aside as the van went racing off.
?!!

CHAPTER FIVE

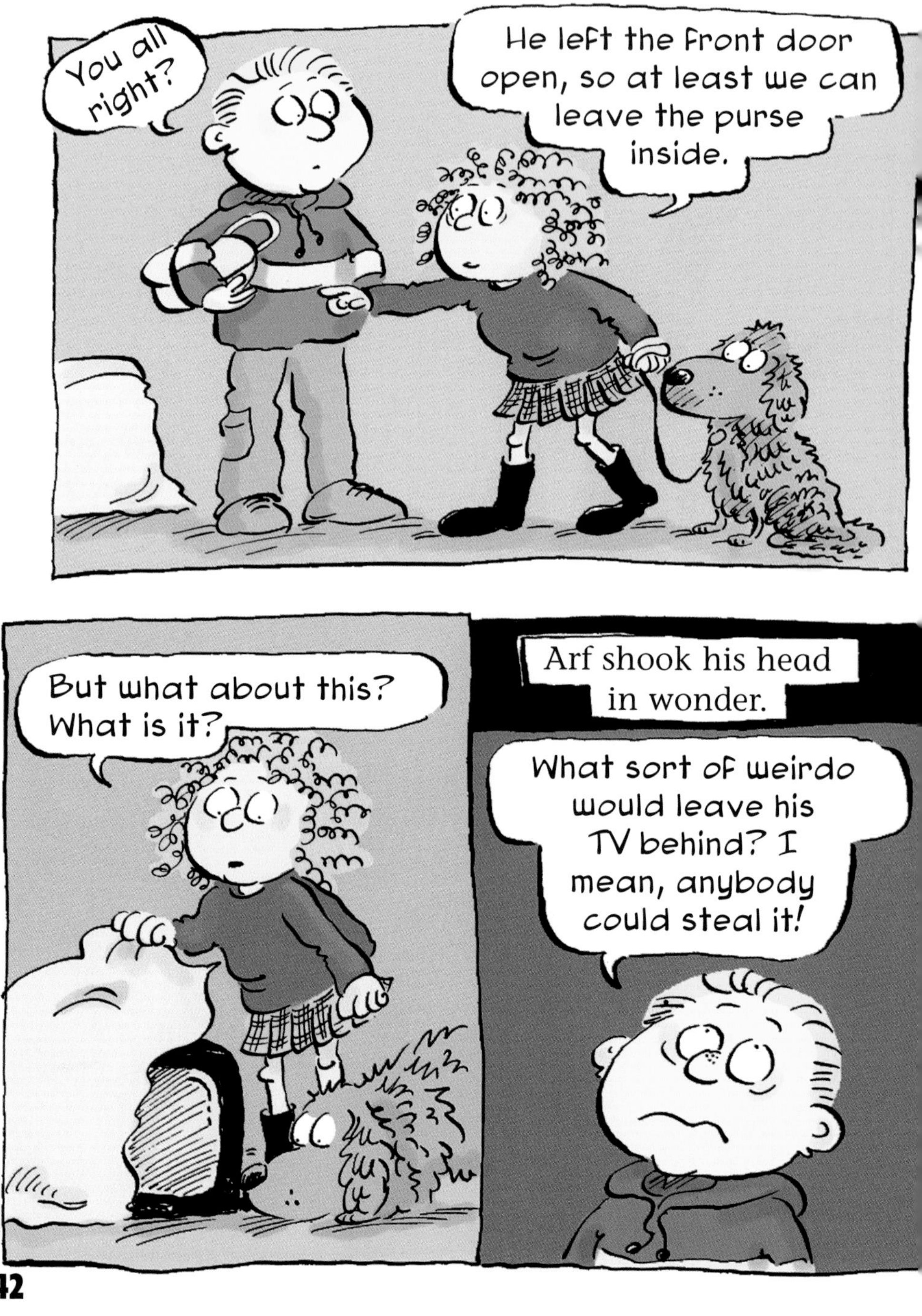
You all right?
He left the front door open, so at least we can leave the purse inside.
But what about this? What is it?
Arf shook his head in wonder.
What sort of weirdo would leave his TV behind? I mean, anybody could steal it!

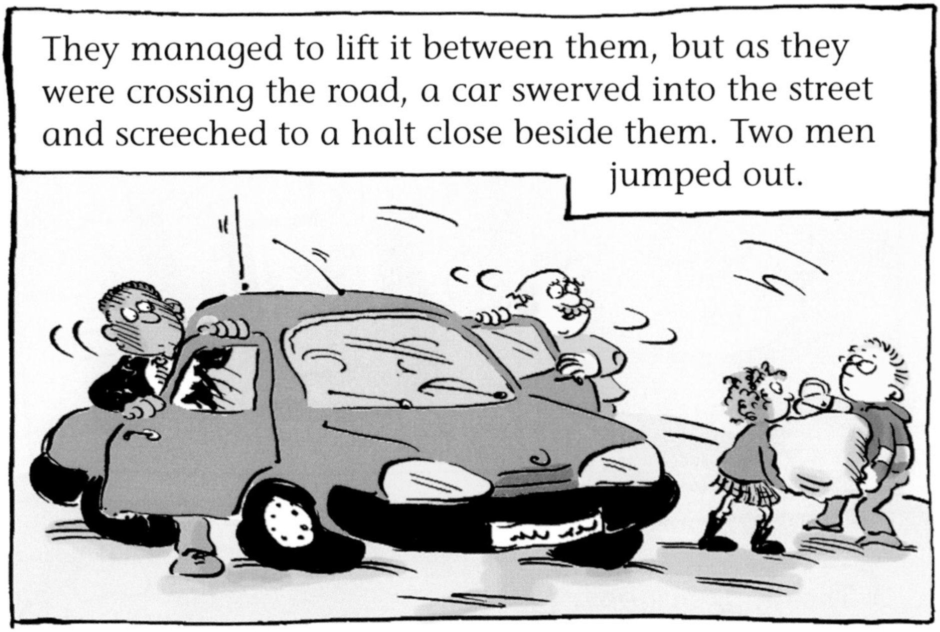
They managed to lift it between them, but as they were crossing the road, a car swerved into the street and screeched to a halt close beside them. Two men jumped out.

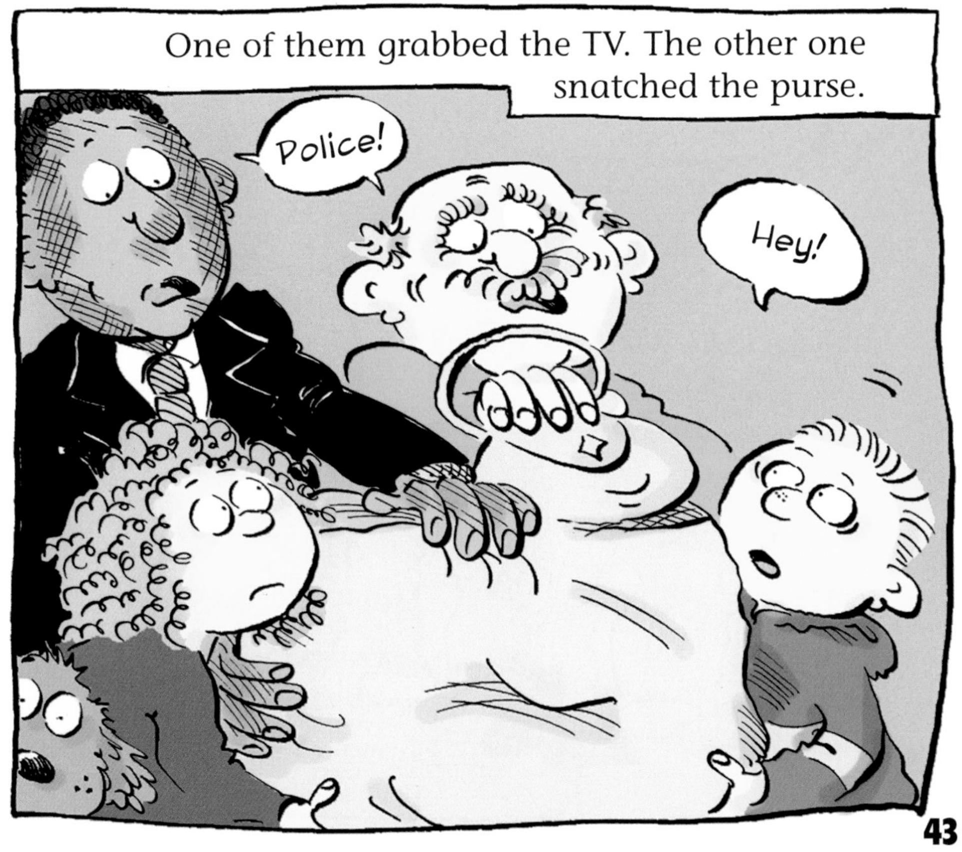
One of them grabbed the TV. The other one snatched the purse.
Police!
Hey!

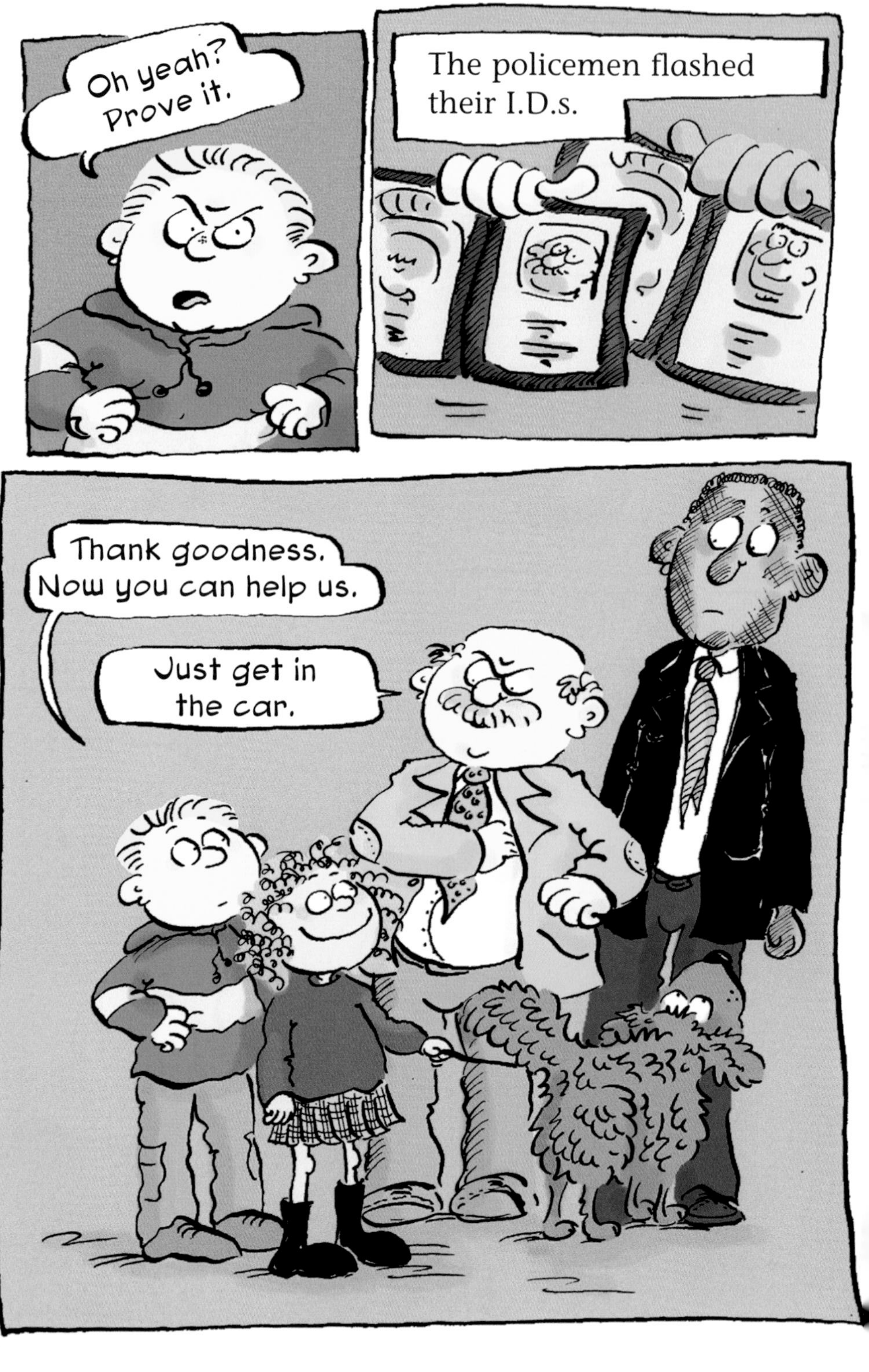
Oh yeah? Prove it.
The policemen flashed their I.D.s.
Thank goodness. Now you can help us.
Just get in the car.

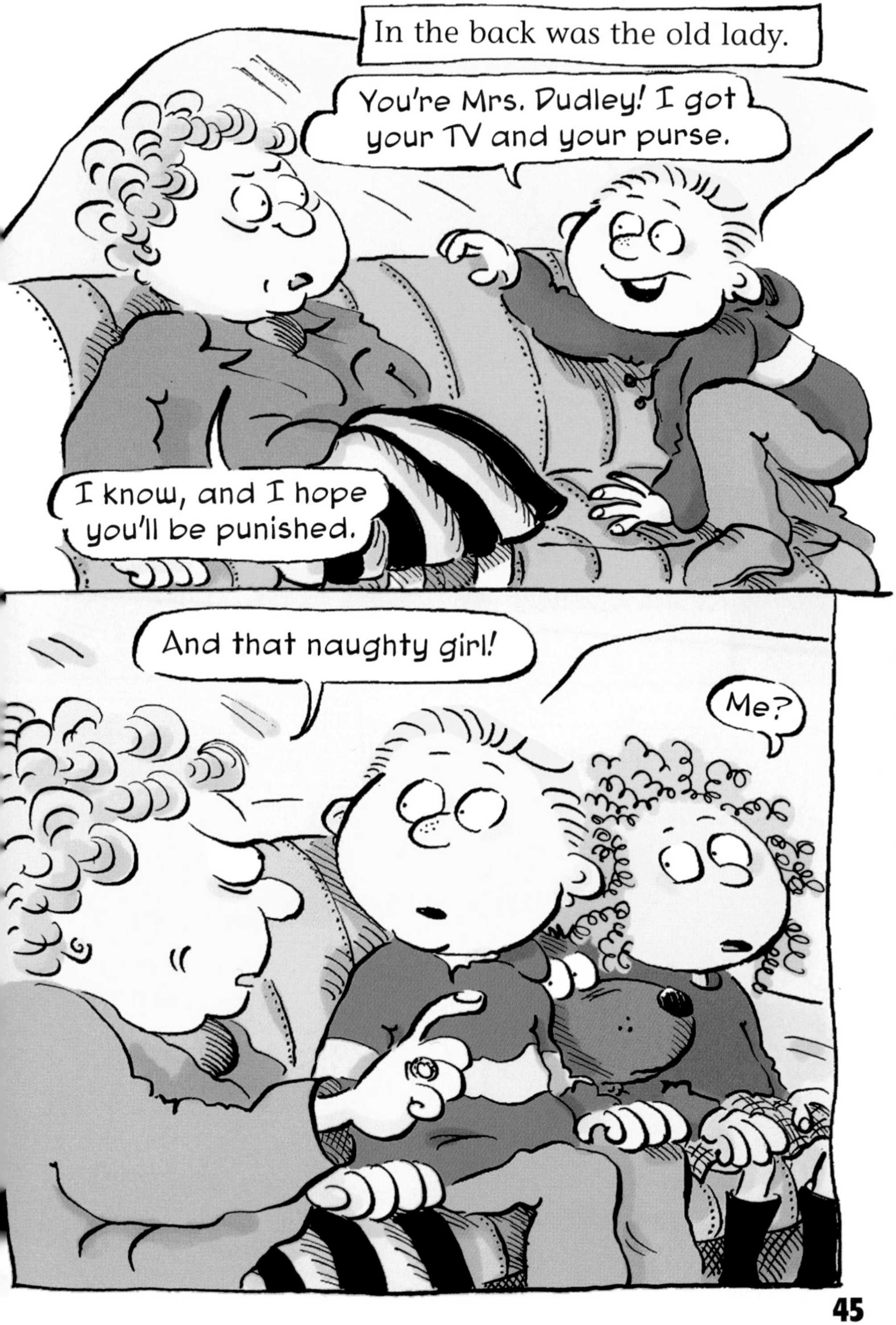
In the back was the old lady.
You're Mrs. Dudley! I got your TV and your purse.
I know, and I hope you'll be punished.
And that naughty girl!
Me?

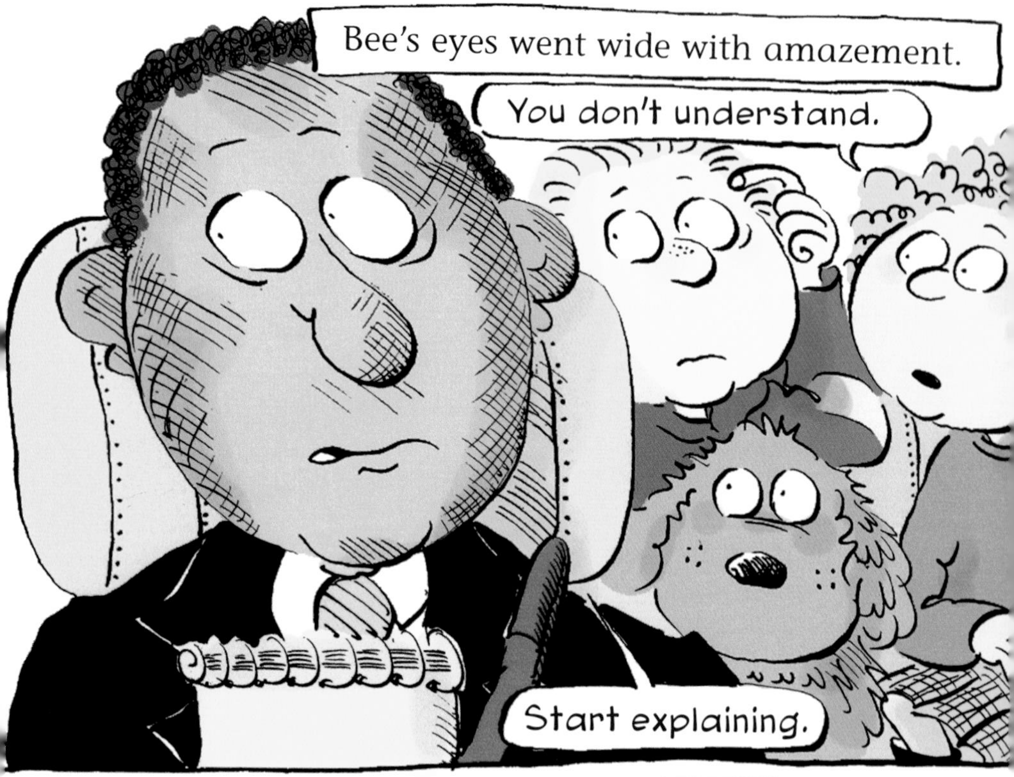
Bee's eyes went wide with amazement.
You don't understand.
Start explaining.

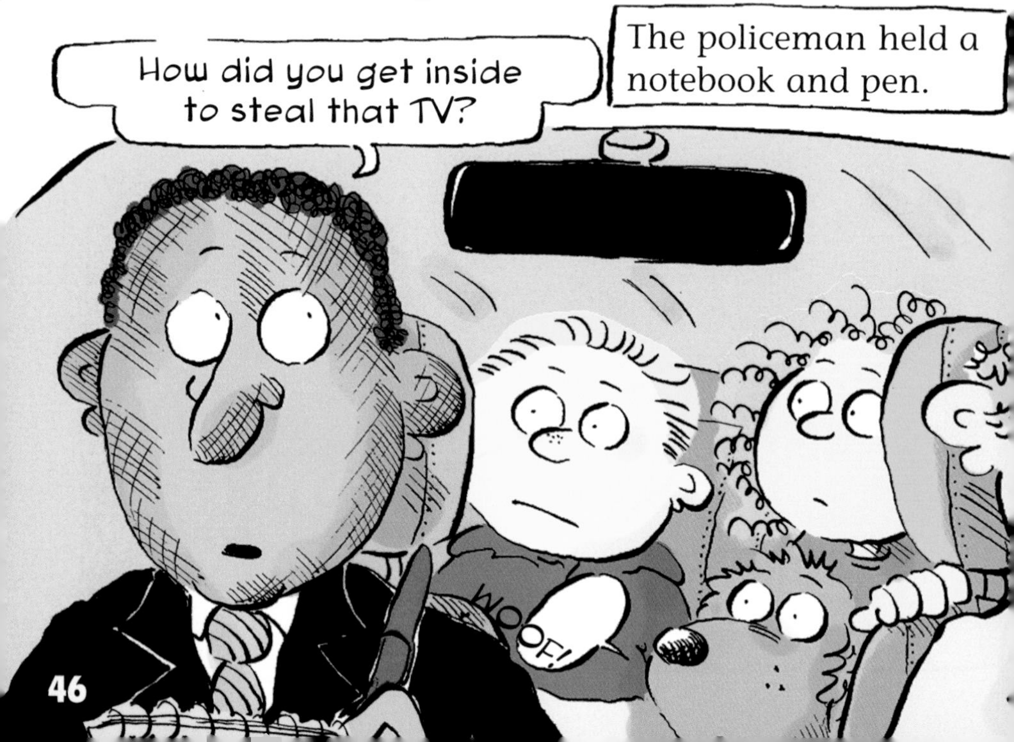
The policeman held a notebook and pen.
How did you get inside to steal that TV?
WOOF!

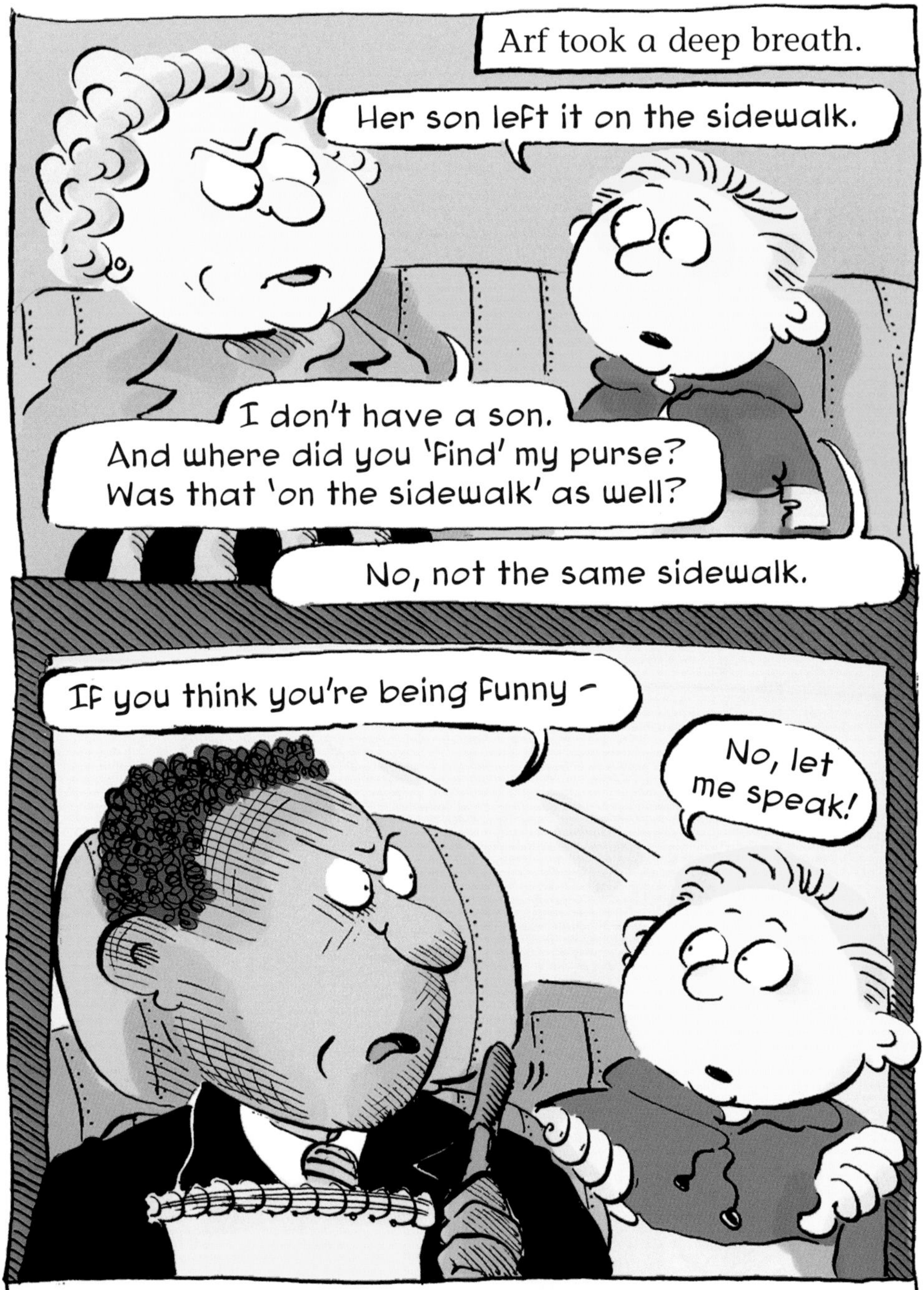
Arf took a deep breath.
Her son left it on the sidewalk.
I don't have a son. And where did you 'find' my purse? Was that 'on the sidewalk' as well?
No, not the same sidewalk.
If you think you're being funny -
No, let me speak!

Arf told them the story about the man stealing his wallet and leaving the purse behind.

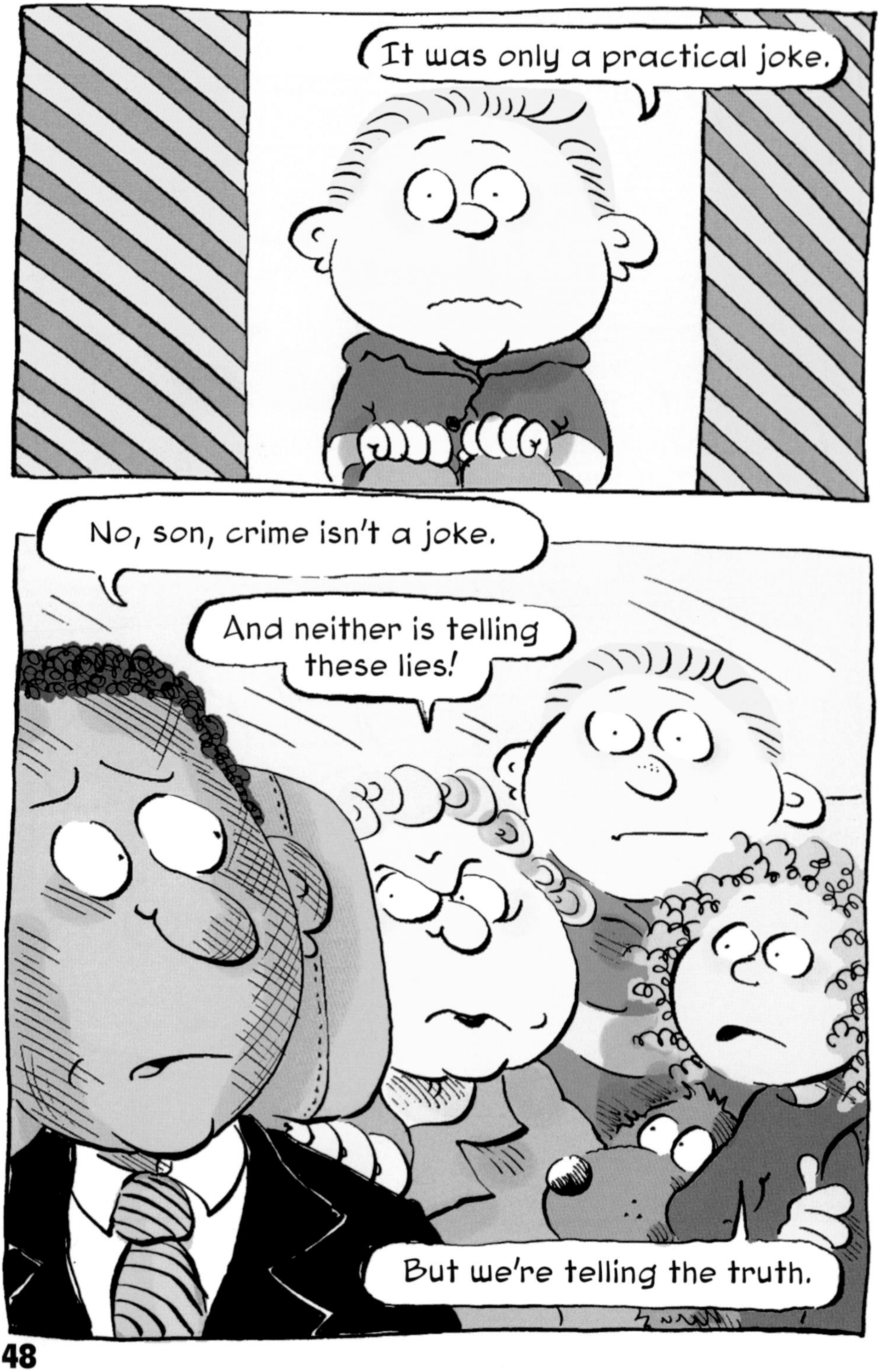

It was only a practical joke.
No, son, crime isn't a joke.
And neither is telling these lies!
But we're telling the truth.

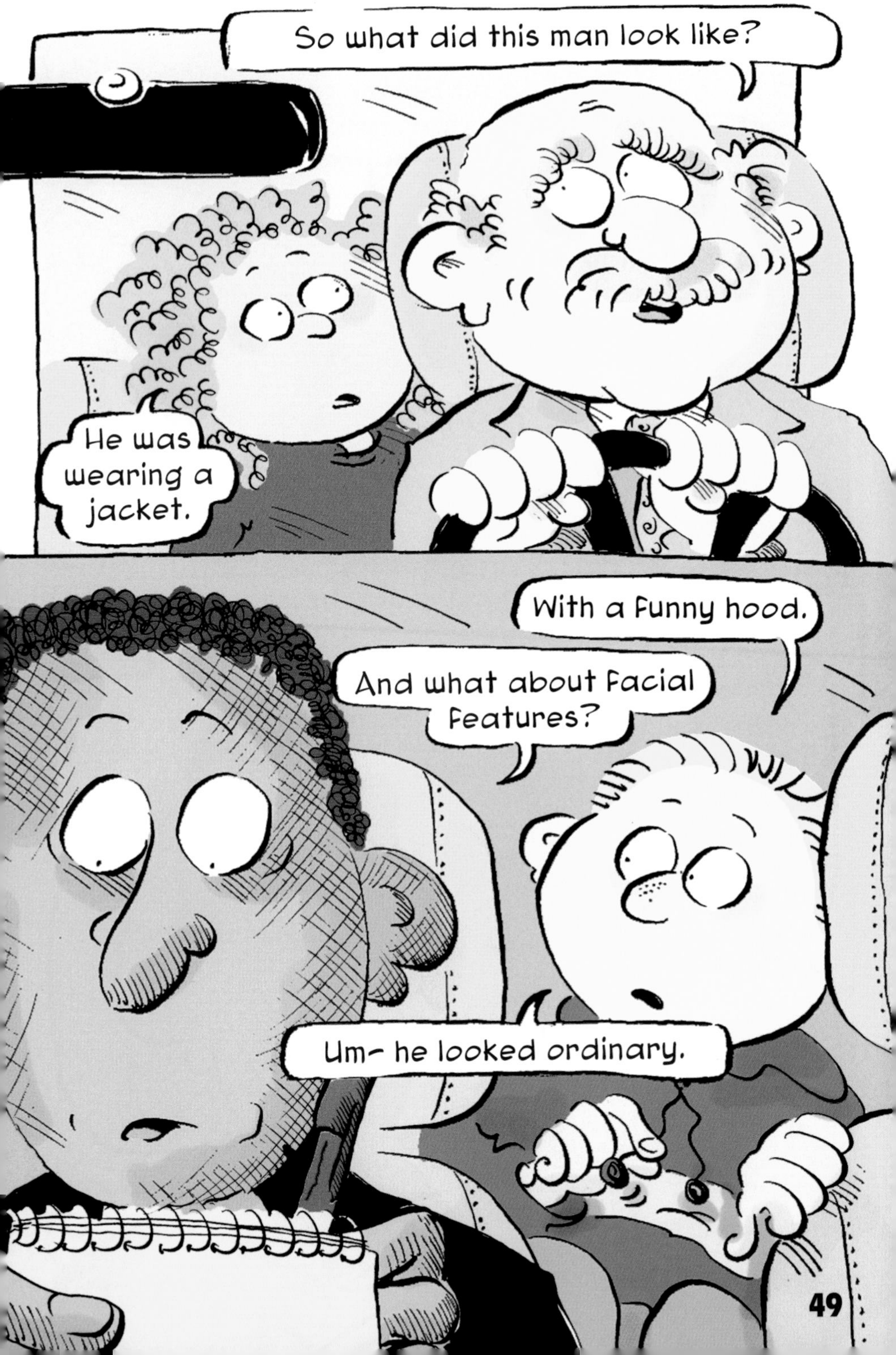
So what did this man look like?
He was wearing a jacket.
With a funny hood.
And what about facial features?
Um- he looked ordinary.

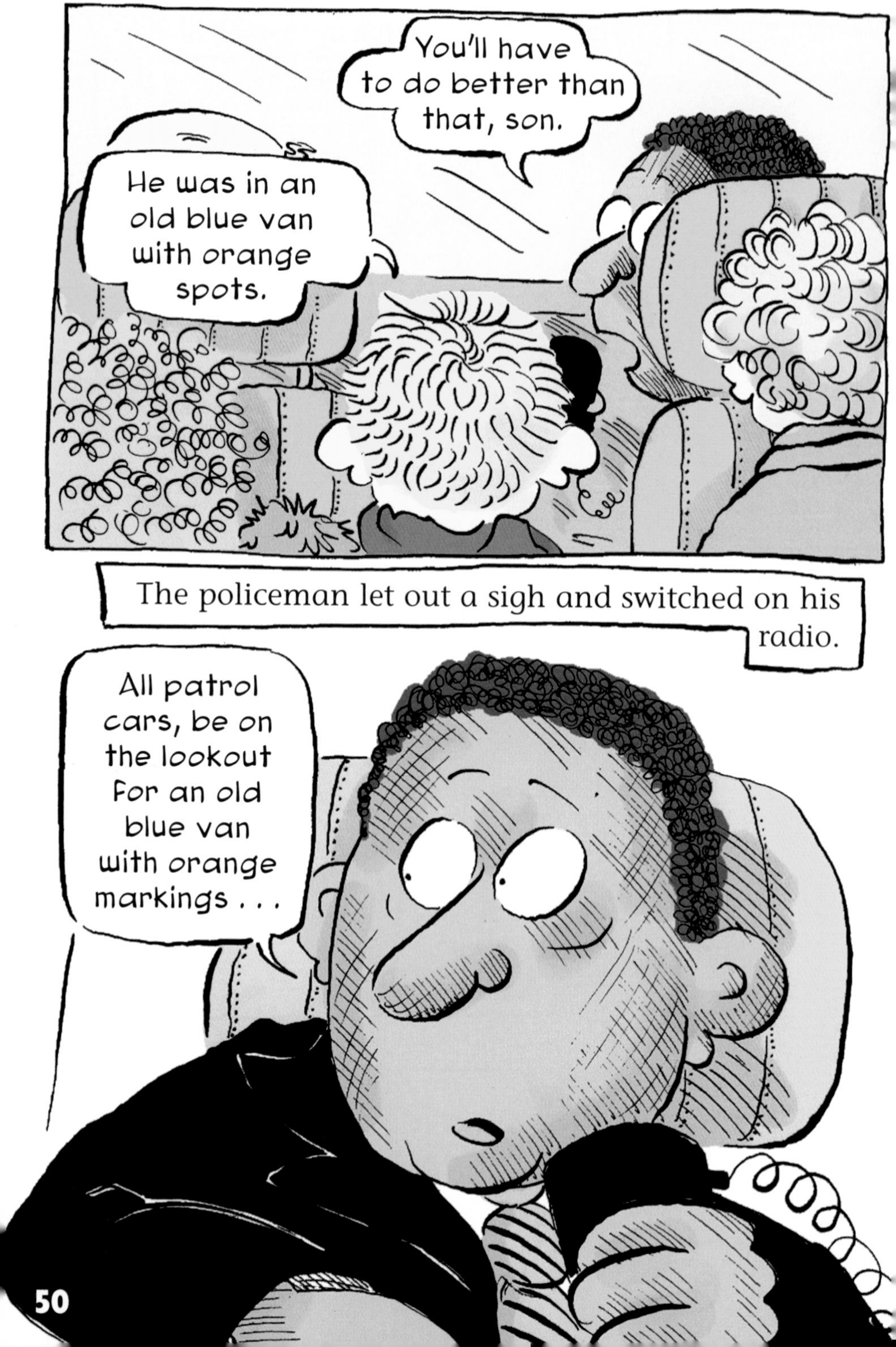
You'll have to do better than that, son.
He was in an old blue van with orange spots.
The policeman let out a sigh and switched on his radio.
All patrol cars, be on the lookout for an old blue van with orange markings . . .

CHAPTER SIX

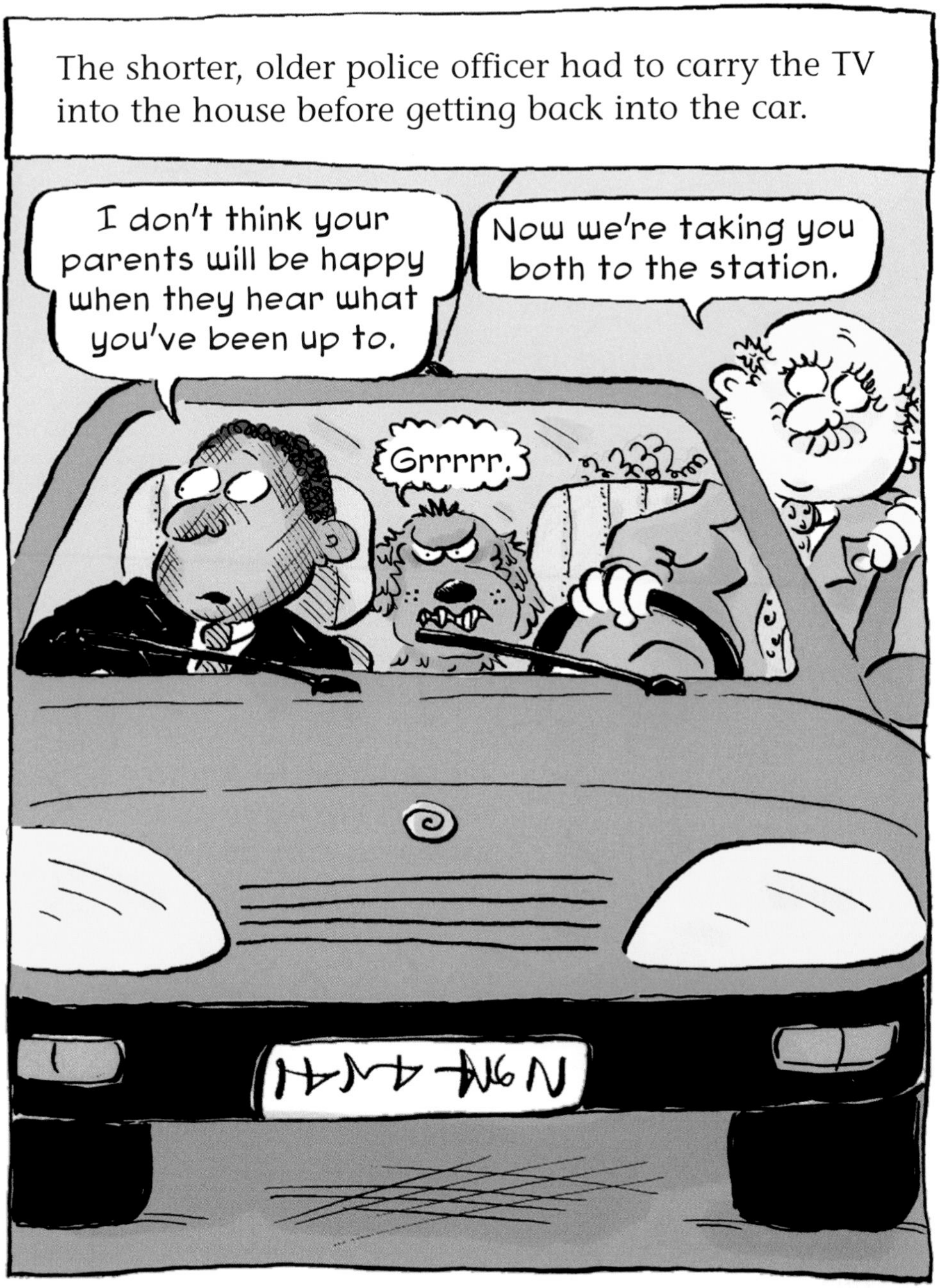
The shorter, older police officer had to carry the TV into the house before getting back into the car.
I don't think your parents will be happy when they hear what you've been up to.
Now we're taking you both to the station.
Grrrrr.

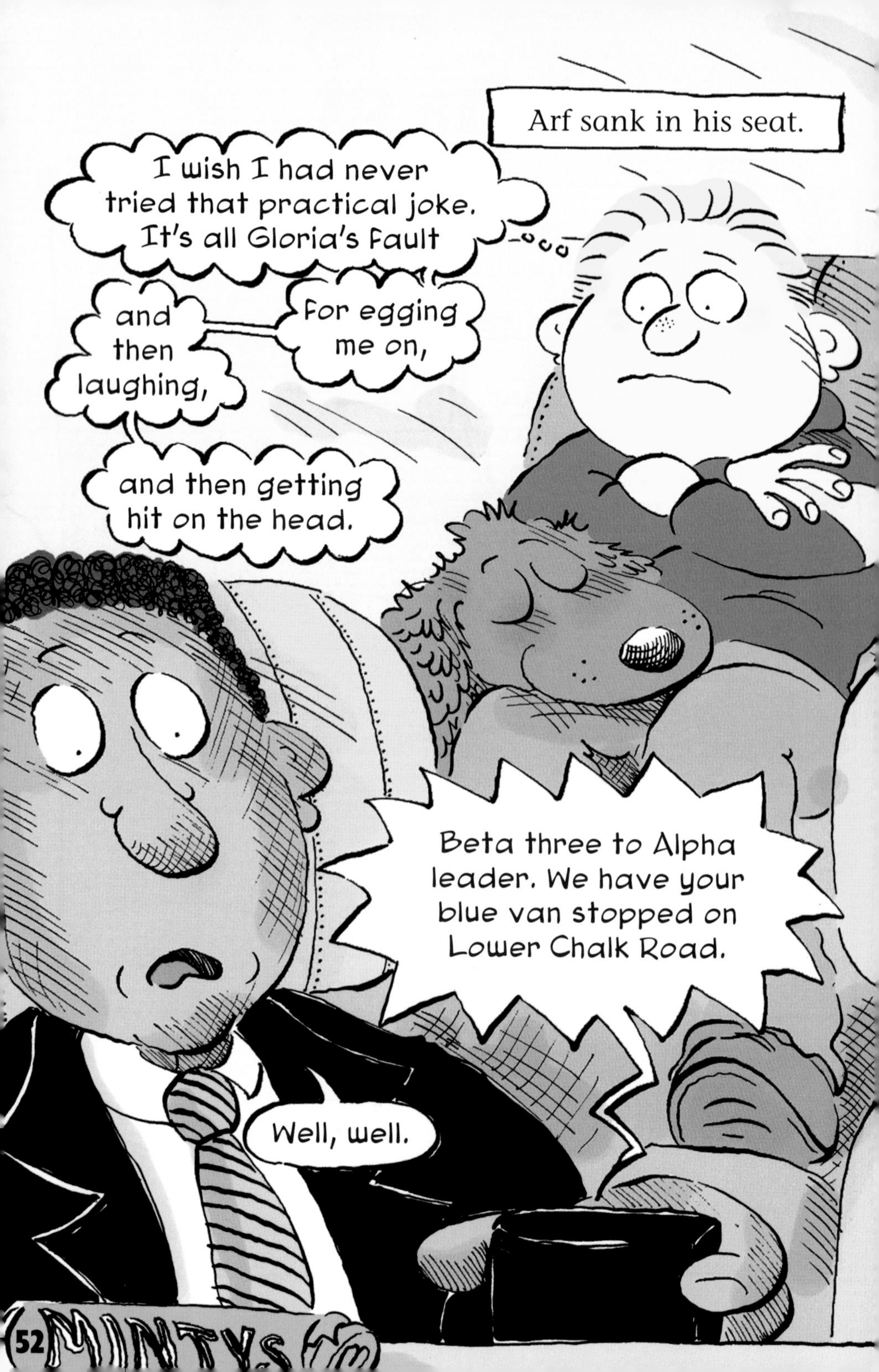
Arf sank in his seat.
I wish I had never tried that practical joke. It's all Gloria's fault
for egging me on,
and then laughing,
and then getting hit on the head.
Beta three to Alpha leader. We have your blue van stopped on Lower Chalk Road.
Well, well.
MINTYS

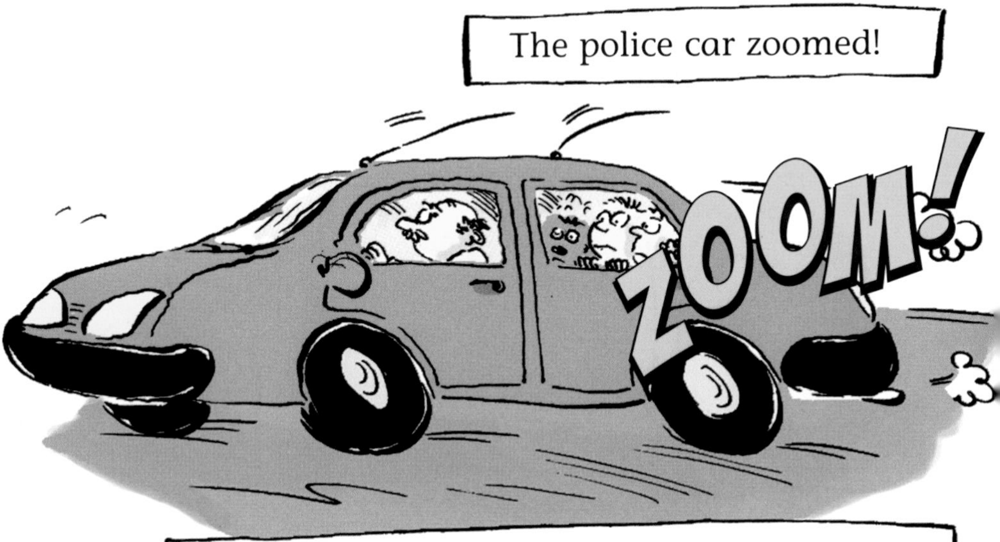
The police car zoomed!
ZOOM!

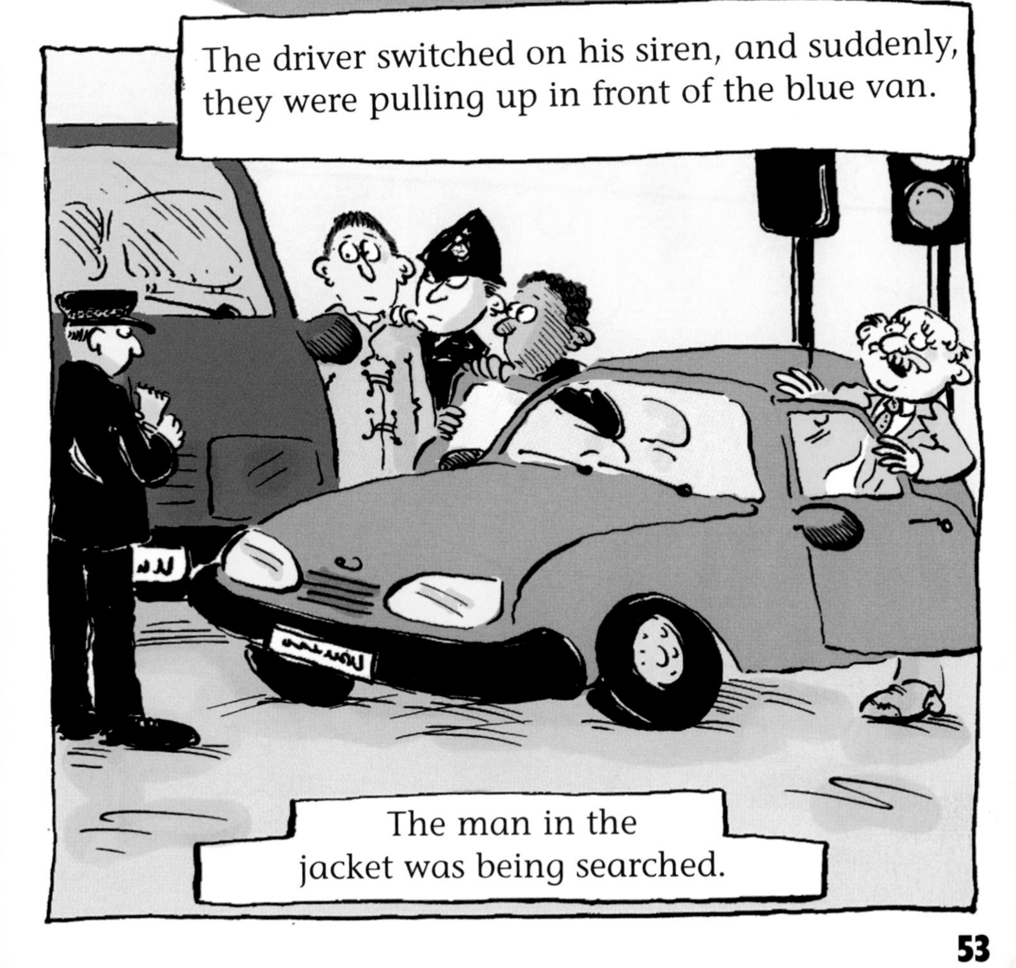
The driver switched on his siren, and suddenly, they were pulling up in front of the blue van.
The man in the jacket was being searched.

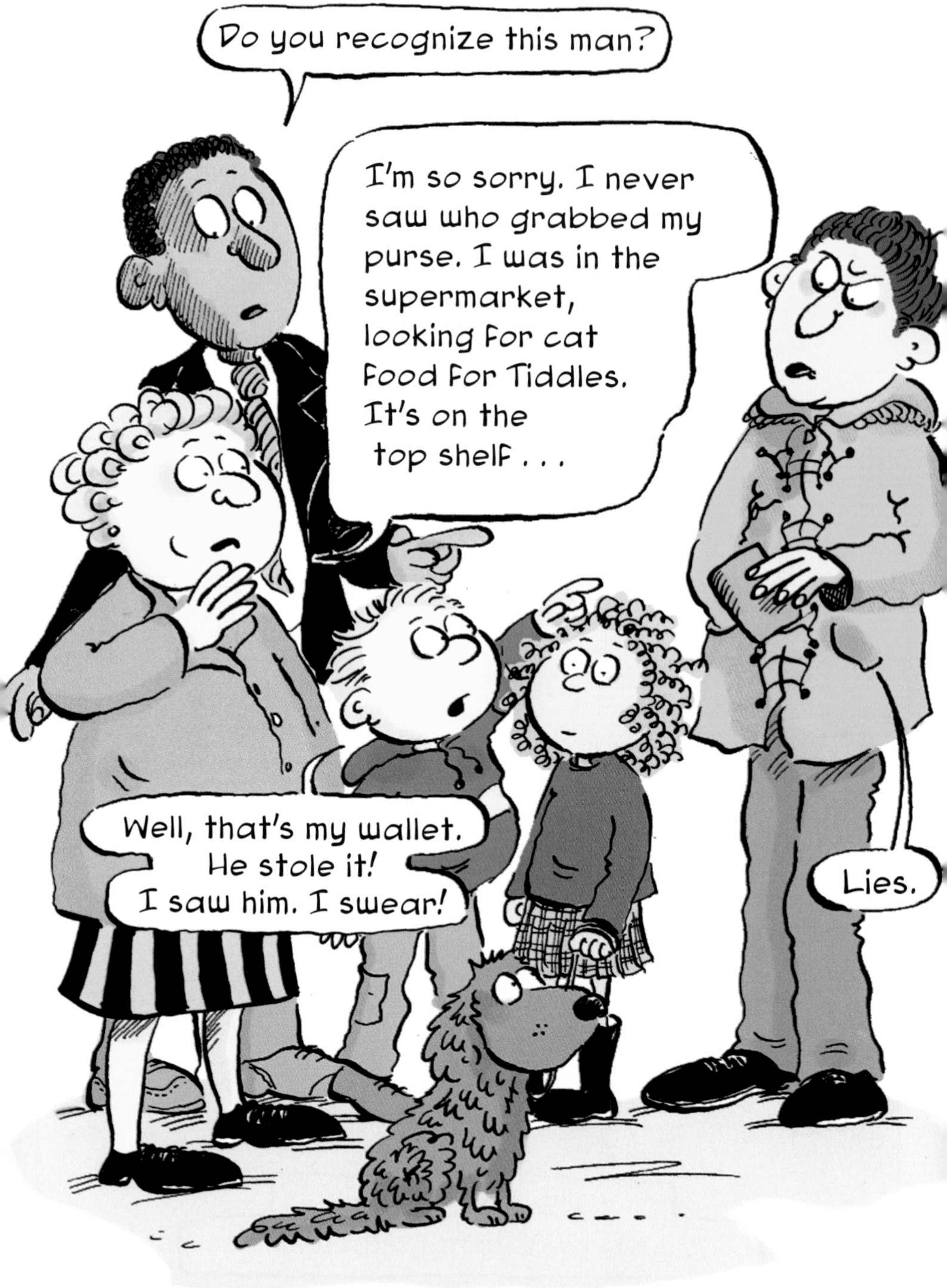
Do you recognize this man?
I'm so sorry. I never saw who grabbed my purse. I was in the supermarket, looking for cat food for Tiddles. It's on the top shelf . . .
Well, that's my wallet. He stole it! I saw him. I swear!
Lies.

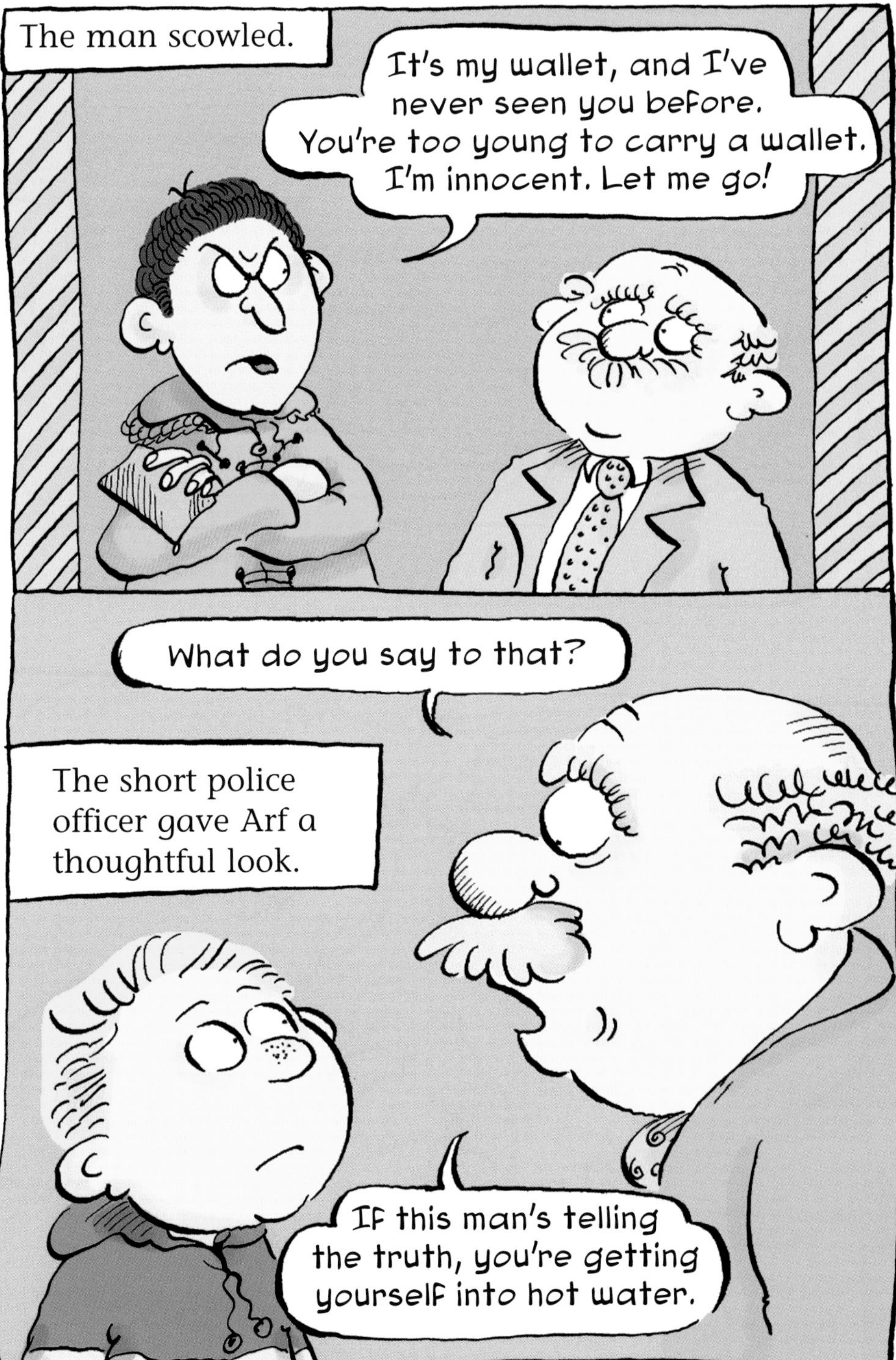
The man scowled.
It's my wallet, and I've never seen you before. You're too young to carry a wallet. I'm innocent. Let me go!
What do you say to that?
The short police officer gave Arf a thoughtful look.
If this man's telling the truth, you're getting yourself into hot water.

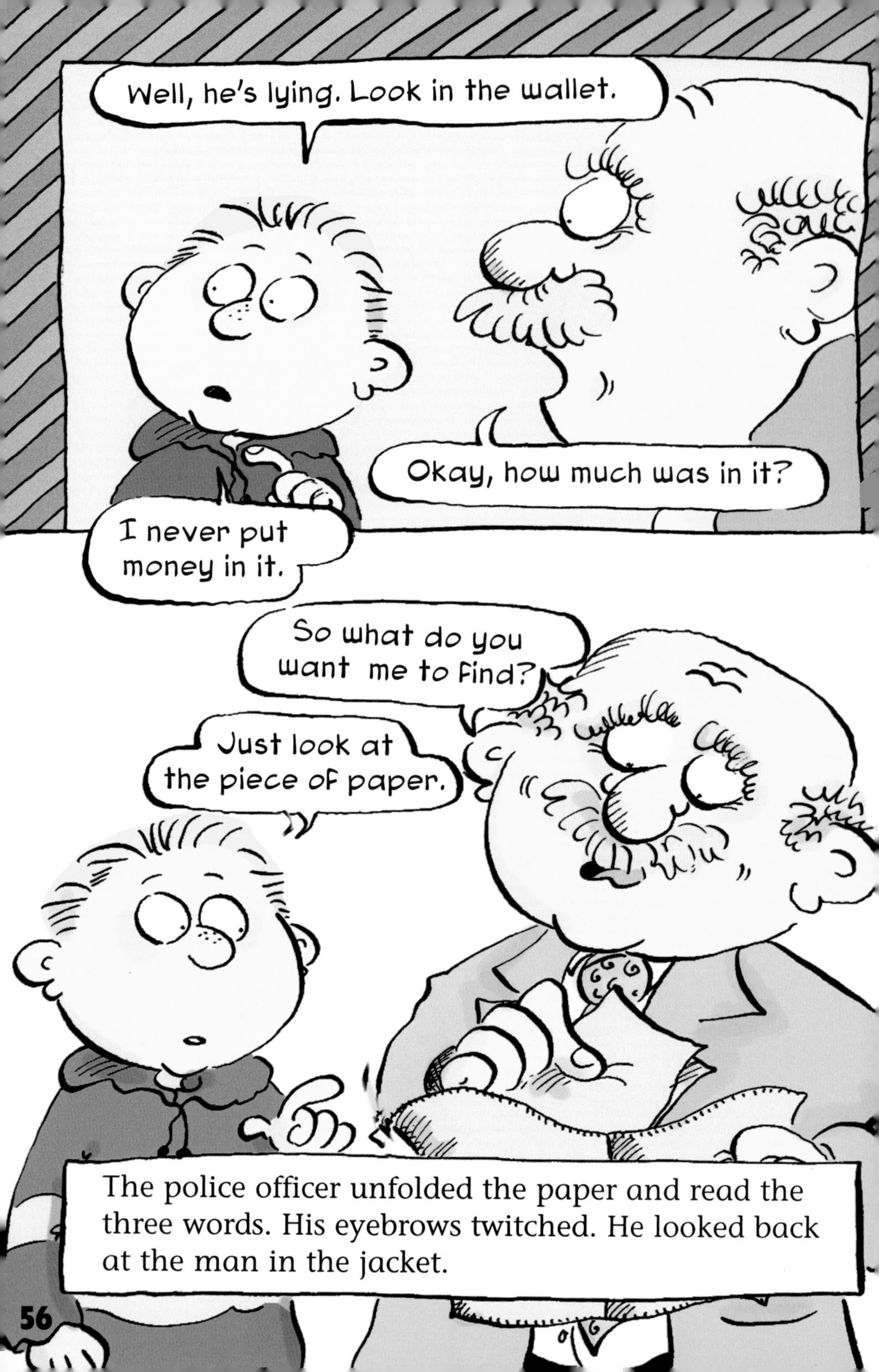
Well, he's lying. Look in the wallet.
Okay, how much was in it?
I never put money in it.
So what do you want me to find?
Just look at the piece of paper.
The police officer unfolded the paper and read the three words. His eyebrows twitched. He looked back at the man in the jacket.

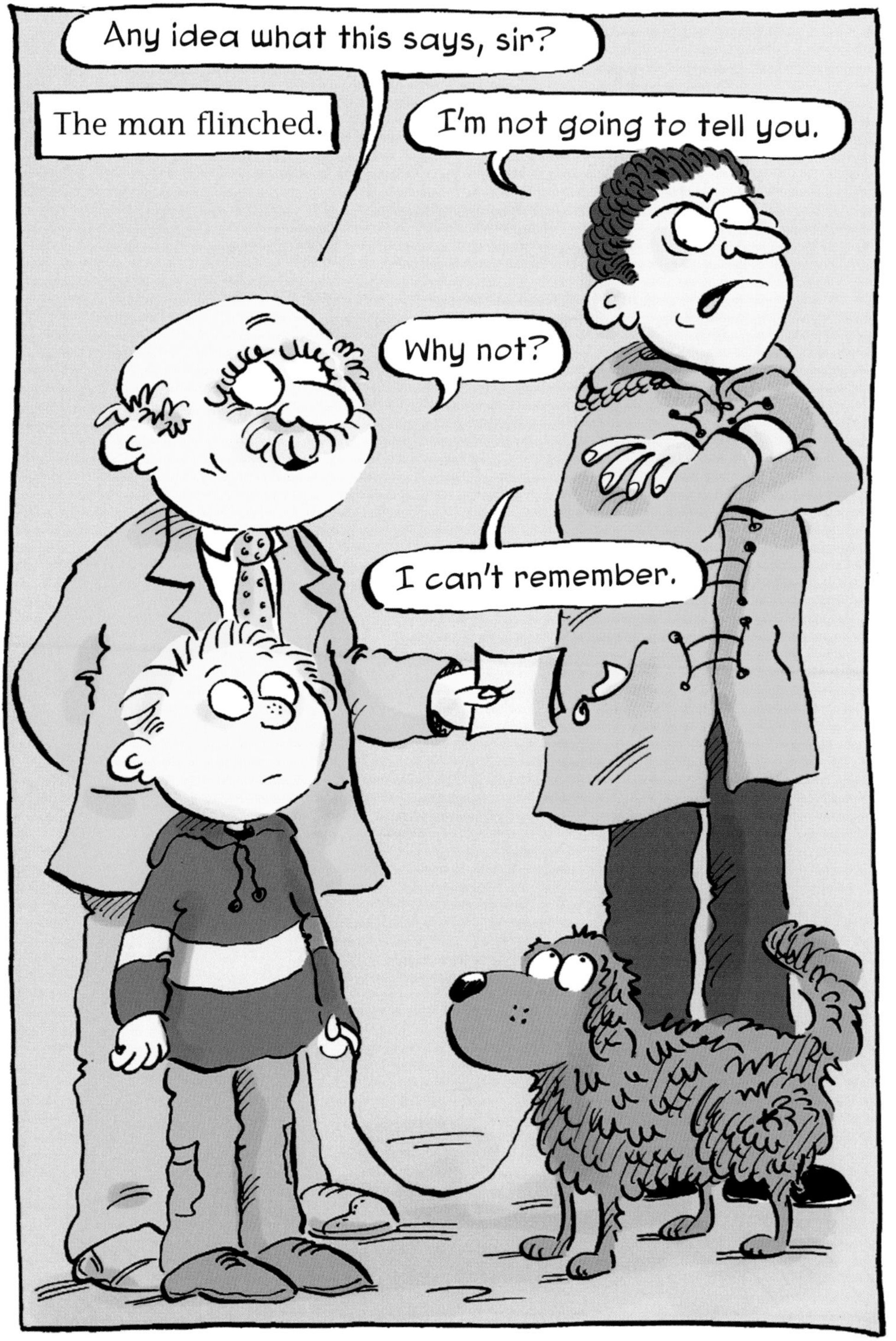
Any idea what this says, sir?
The man flinched.
I'm not going to tell you.
Why not?
I can't remember.

Everyone turned to Arf, who stared the man straight in the face.

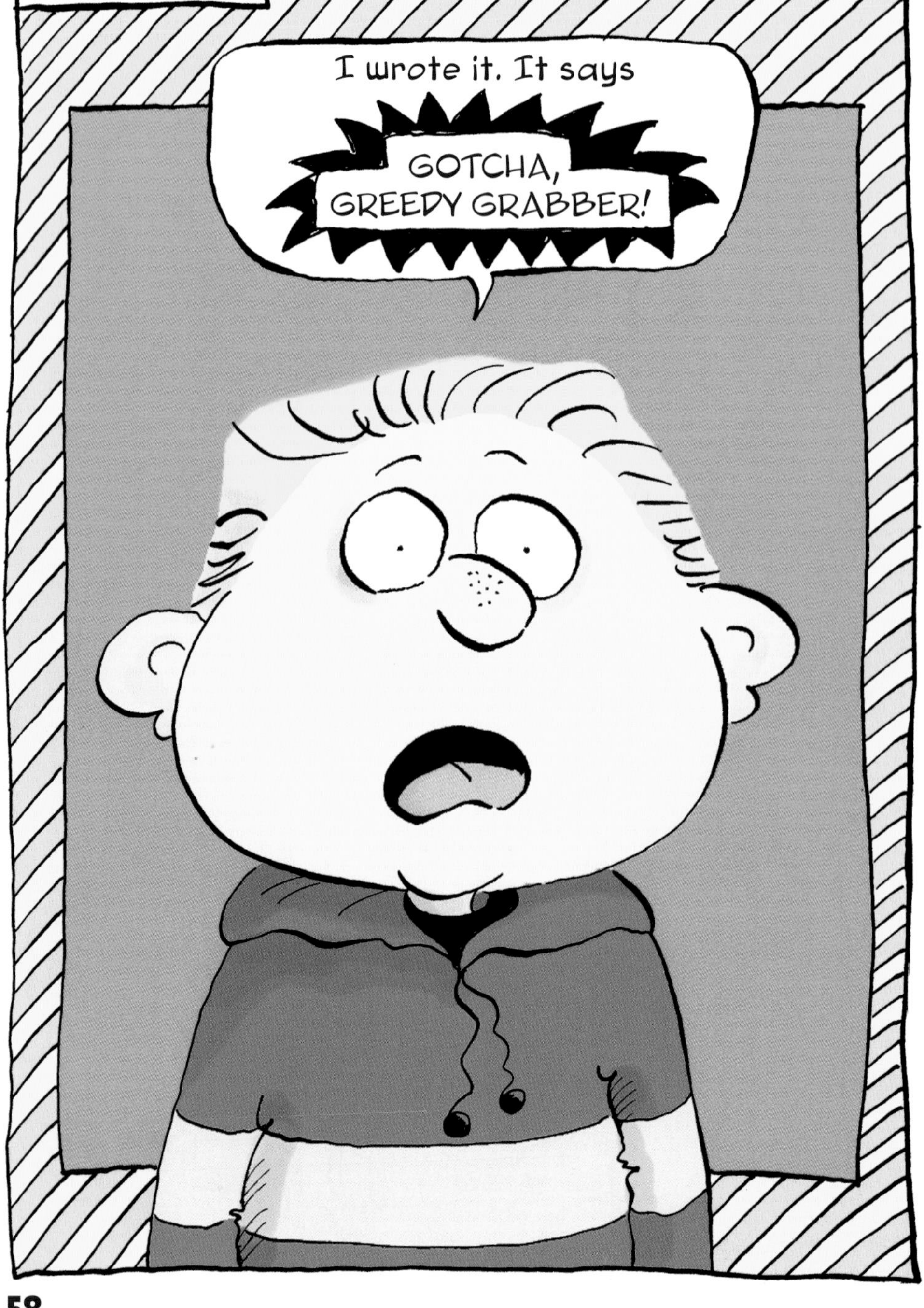
I wrote it. It says
GOTCHA, GREEDY GRABBER!

The man looked like a drowned goldfish.

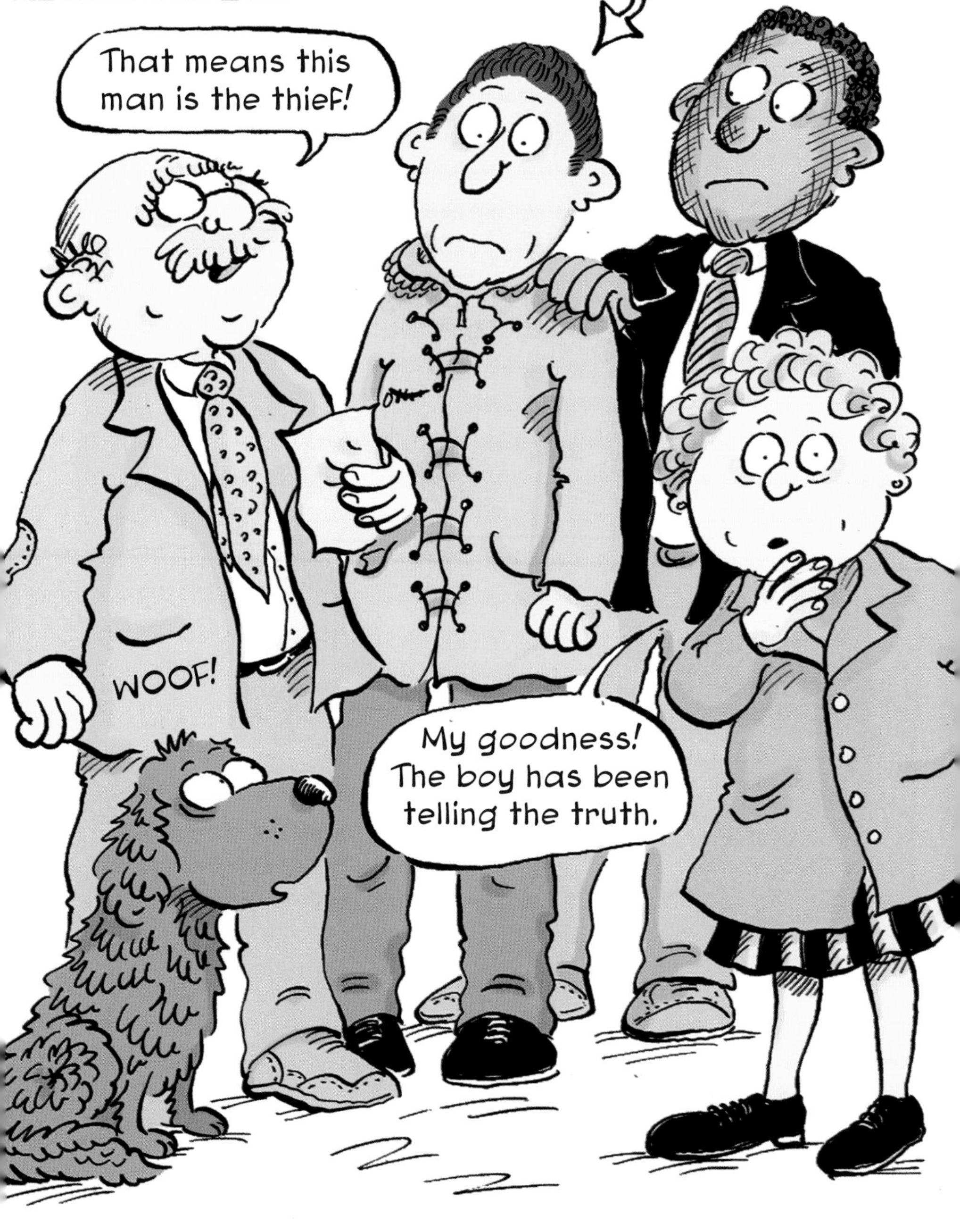
That means this man is the thief!
WOOF!
My goodness! The boy has been telling the truth.

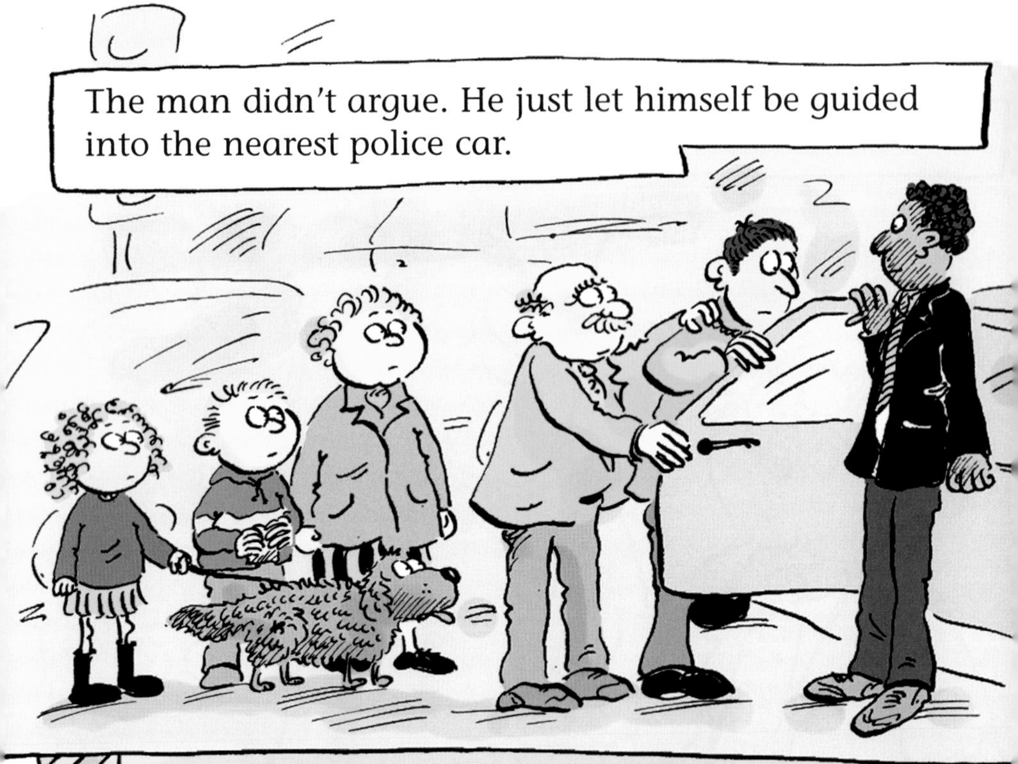
The man didn't argue. He just let himself be guided into the nearest police car.

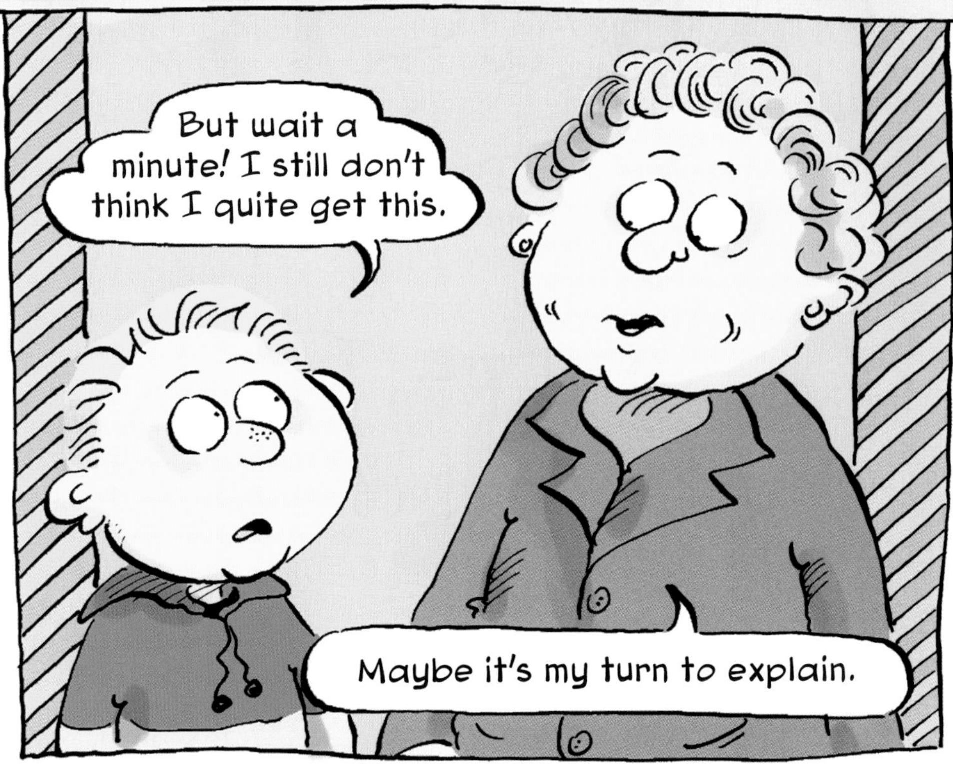
But wait a minute! I still don't think I quite get this.
Maybe it's my turn to explain.

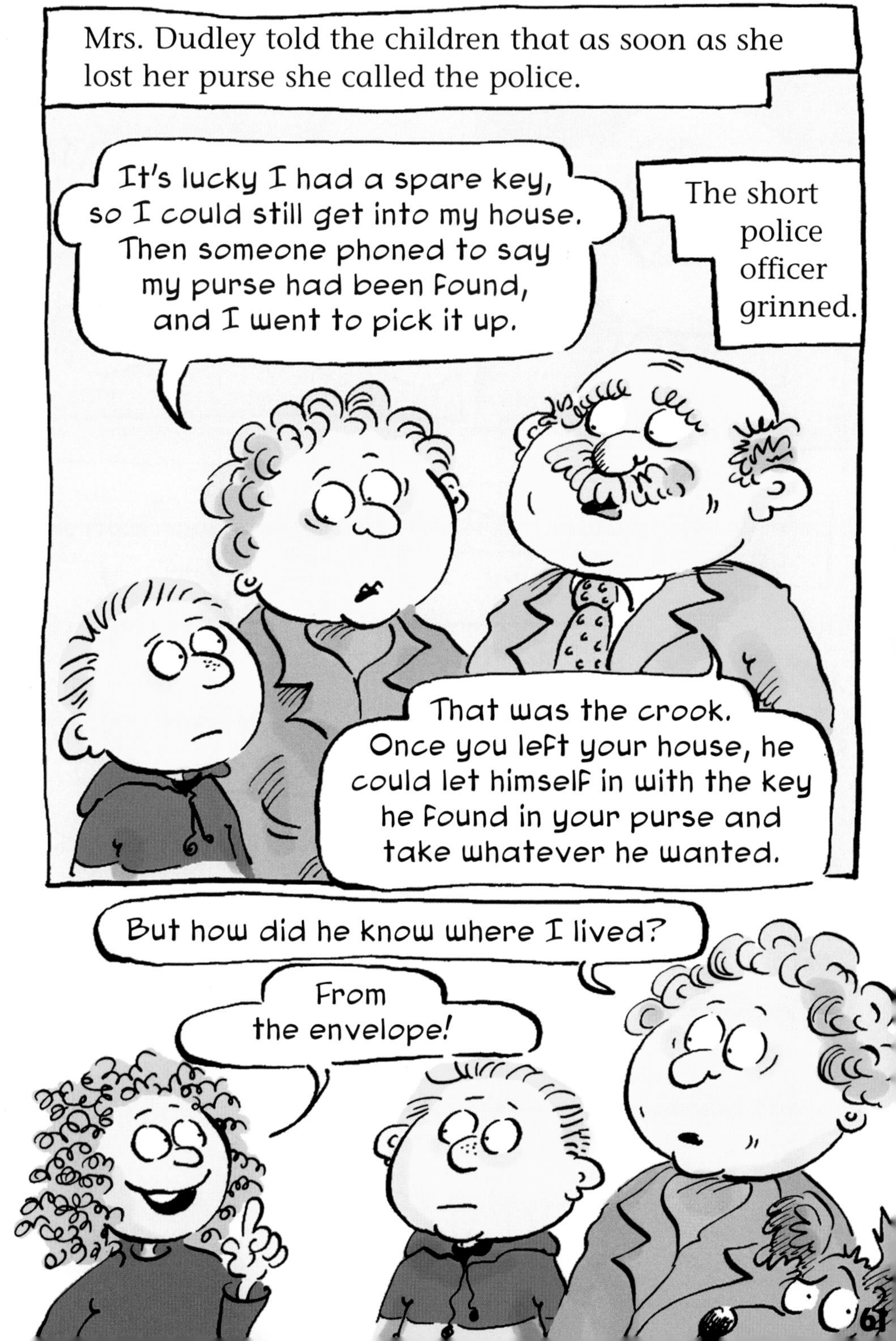
Mrs. Dudley told the children that as soon as she lost her purse she called the police.
It's lucky I had a spare key, so I could still get into my house. Then someone phoned to say my purse had been found, and I went to pick it up.
The short police officer grinned.
That was the crook. Once you left your house, he could let himself in with the key he found in your purse and take whatever he wanted.
But how did he know where I lived?
From the envelope!

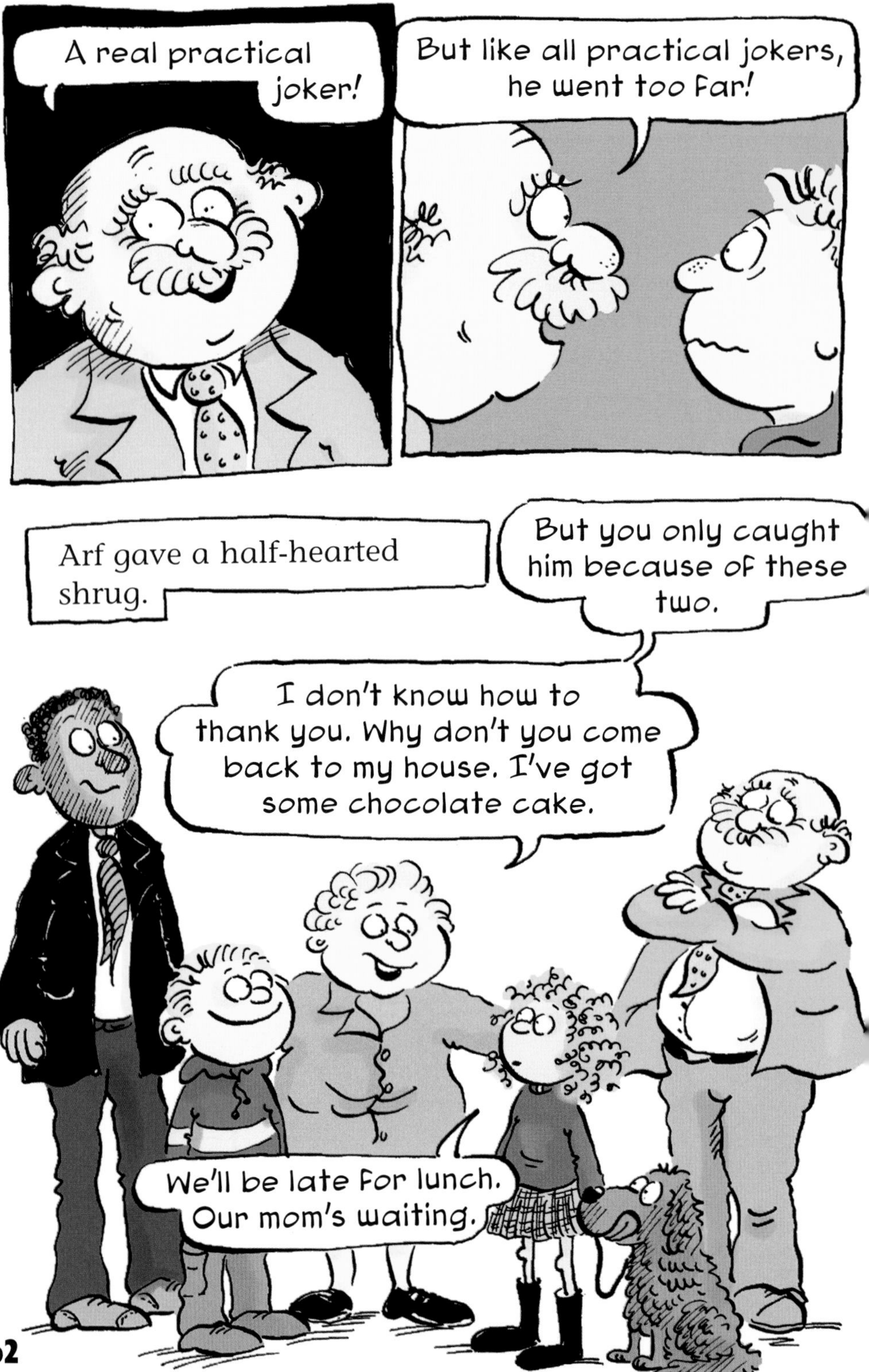
A real practical joker!
But like all practical jokers, he went too far!
Arf gave a half-hearted shrug.
But you only caught him because of these two.
I don't know how to thank you. Why don't you come back to my house. I've got some chocolate cake.
We'll be late for lunch. Our mom's waiting.

CHAPTER SEVEN

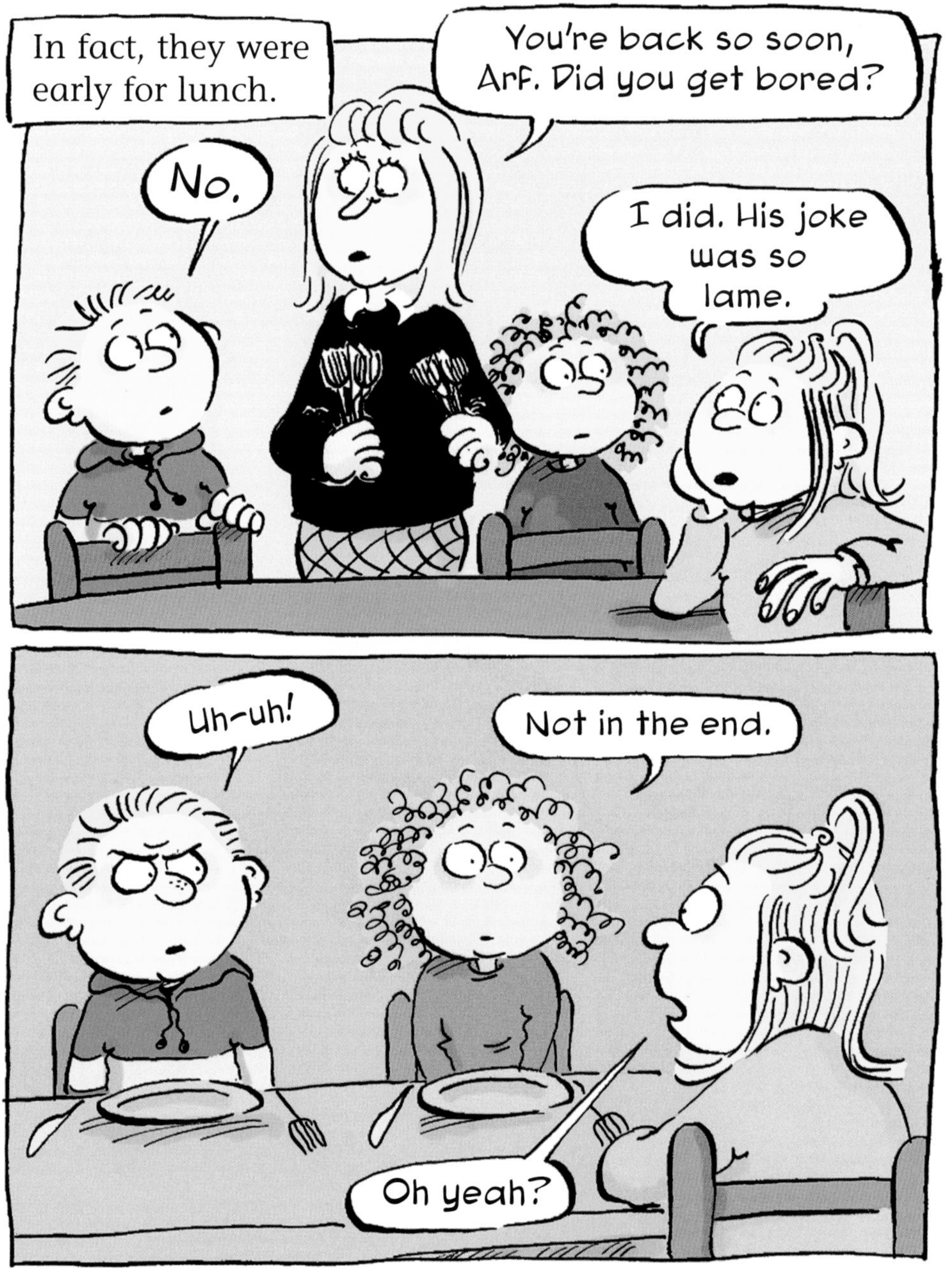
In fact, they were early for lunch.
You're back so soon, Arf. Did you get bored?
No.
I did. His joke was so lame.
Uh-uh!
Not in the end.
Oh yeah?

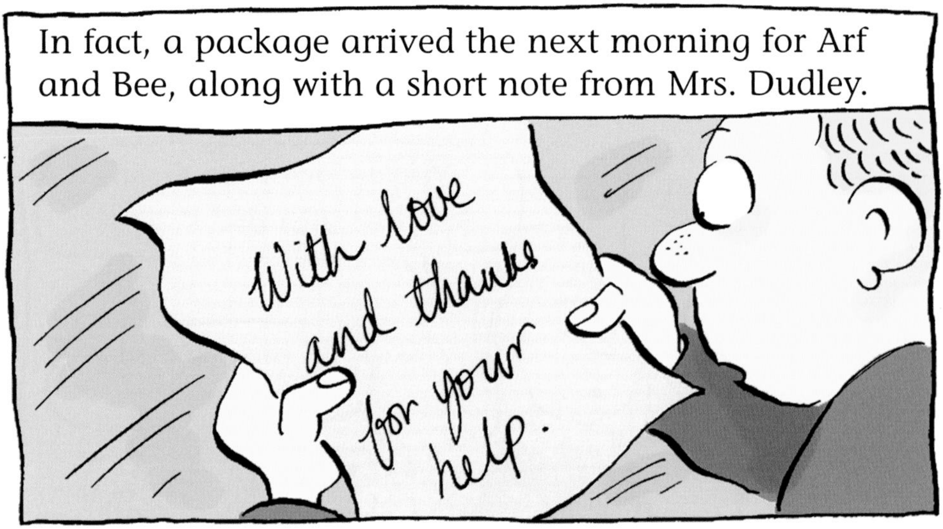
In fact, a package arrived the next morning for Arf and Bee, along with a short note from Mrs. Dudley.
With love and thanks for your help.

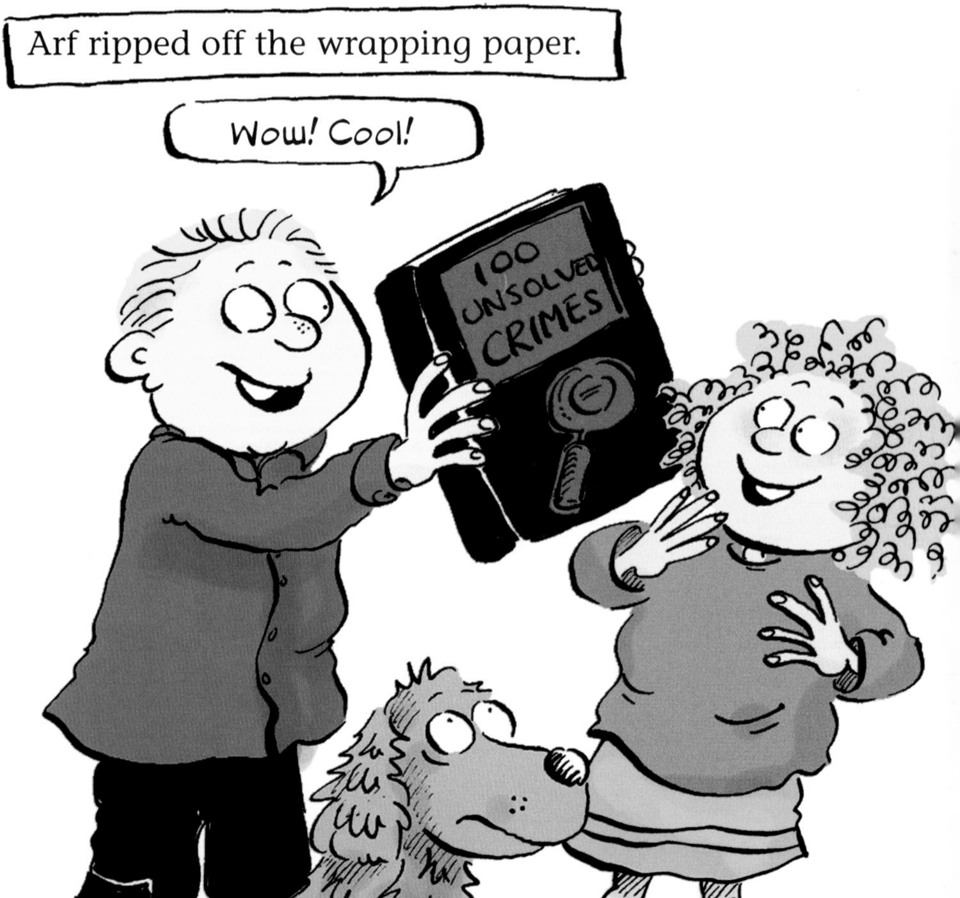
Arf ripped off the wrapping paper.
Wow! Cool!
100 UNSOLVED CRIMES

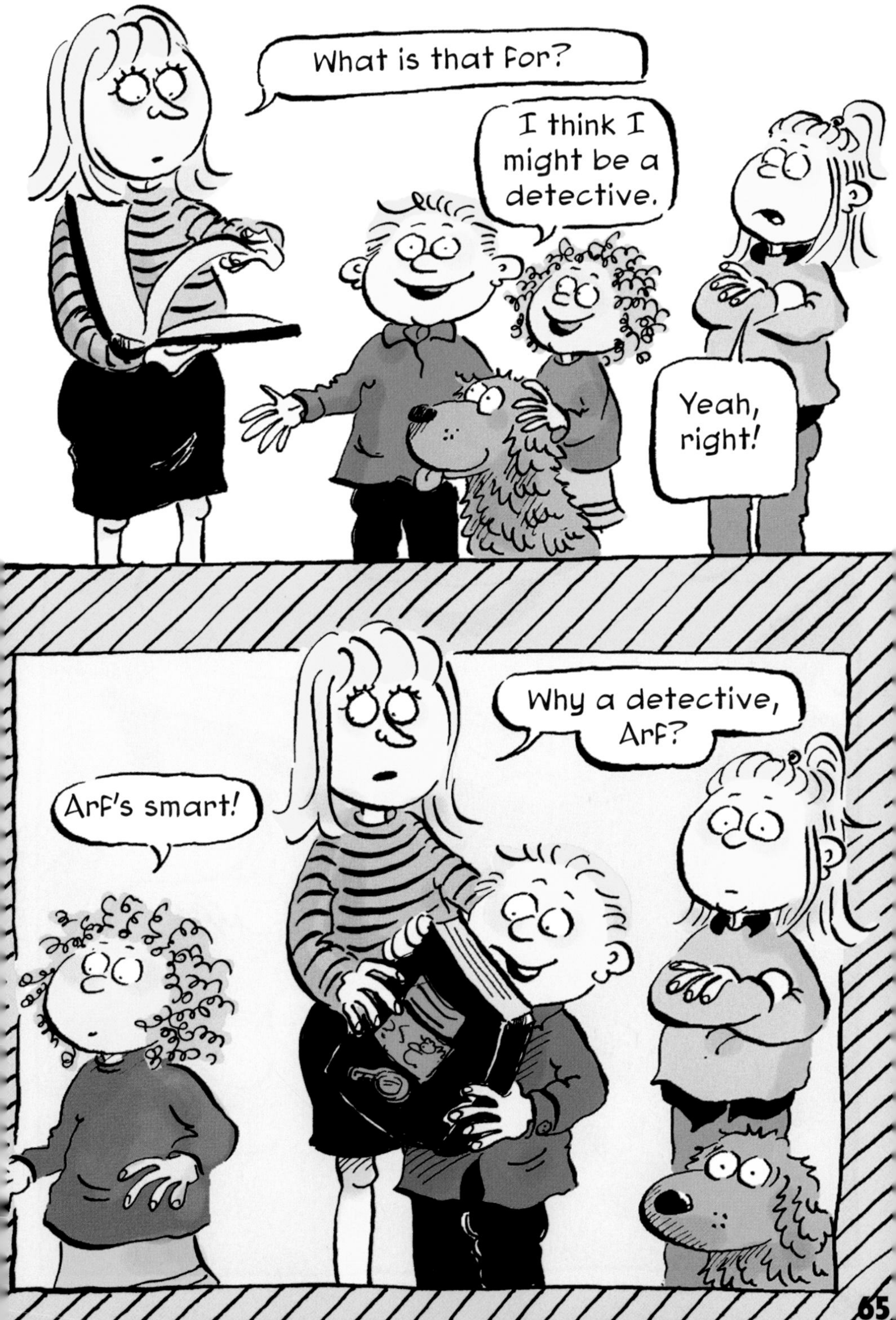
What is that for?
I think I might be a detective.
Yeah, right!
Arf's smart!
Why a detective, Arf?

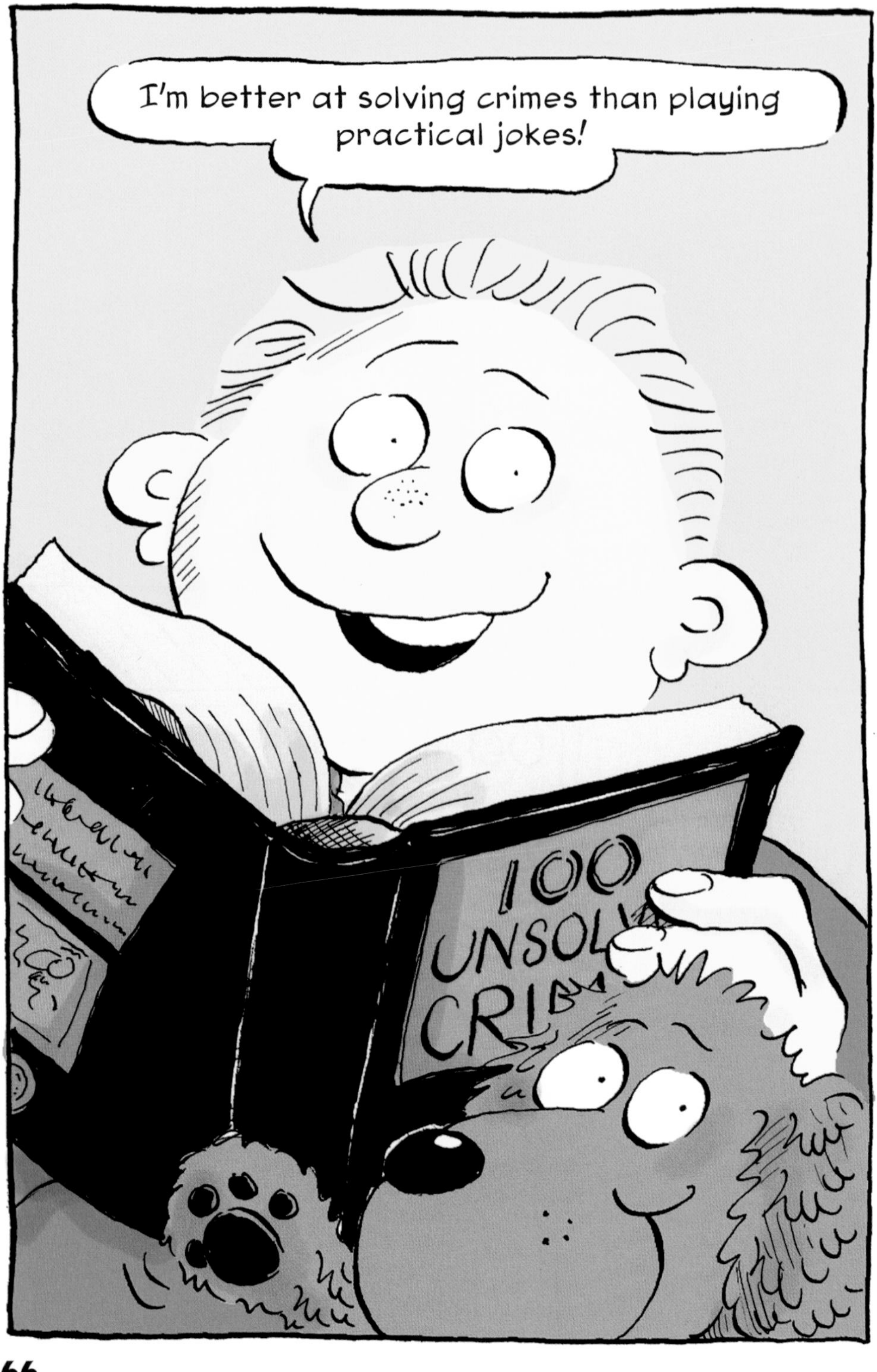
I'm better at solving crimes than playing practical jokes!
100 UNSOL CRI

ABOUT THE AUTHOR

Philip Wooderson lives in England. He has written more than 20 books for children.

ABOUT THE ILLUSTRATOR

Bridget MacKeith has illustrated more than 30 books for children. She lives with her husband, two children, and a big, hairy dog in Wiltshire, England. She likes swimming and walking when she isn't busy painting and drawing.

GLOSSARY

convince (kun-VINSS)—to make someone believe something

crook (KRUK)—a person who commits crimes

detective (di-TEK-tiv)—a person who solves crimes

I.D. card (EYE DEE KARD)—a card with your name and picture on it

patiently (PAY-shunt-lee)—to act calmly while putting up with problems

practical (PRAK-tuh-kul)—useful

practical joke (PRAK-tuh-kul joke)—a trick that makes someone look foolish

scowl (SKOWL)—to make an angry frown

INTERNET SITES

Do you want to know more about subjects related to this book? Or are you interested in learning about other topics? Then check out FactHound, a fun, easy way to find Internet sites.

Our investigative staff has already sniffed out great sites for you!

Here's how to use FactHound:

1. Visit *www.facthound.com*

2. Select your grade level.

3. To learn more about subjects related to this book, type in the book's ISBN number: **1598890220**.

4. Click the **Fetch It** button.

FactHound will fetch the best Internet sites for you.

DISCUSSION QUESTIONS

1. At the end of the story, Arf says that he wants to solve crimes instead of play jokes. Do you think Arf has really finished playing jokes on his family, friends, and neighbors? Why or why not?

2. Why does Arf decide to return the purse to Mrs. Dudley instead of turning it in to the police?

3. When Arf described the thief to the police, he said the man was ordinary looking. Luckily, he remembered what the man's van looked like. What are different ways you can describe a person? Think about how they act, talk, and look.

WRITING PROMPTS

1. Do you like to play practical jokes? If you could play any kind of practical joke on your friends, without anyone getting hurt, what joke would you play? Write about the joke and how it works.

2. Write what you would do if you found a purse on the sidewalk. Would you turn it in to the police or try to find its owner?

3. Arf and Bee were accused of stealing Mrs. Dudley's purse and TV. Have you ever been accused of something that you did not do? Write about what happened. Were you able to convince people that you were not guilty?

ALSO PUBLISHED BY STONE ARCH BOOKS

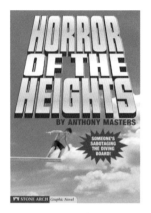

Horror of the Heights
by Anthony Masters
1-59889-030-1

Dean suffers from a fear of heights — a big deal if your brother is a diving champion. Someone is out to sabotage the diving board that Dean fears. Can he expose the saboteur?

Hit It!
by Michael Hardcastle
1-59889-027-1

Scott and Kel are rivals on the same soccer team, the Aces. As they compete to be the team's top scorer, their team chases after the league championship. Scott and Kel need to decide what's more important, their personal goals or teamwork.

STONE ARCH BOOKS,
151 Good Counsel Hill Drive, Mankato, MN 56001
1-800-421-7731
www.stonearchbooks.com